T0130007

A
DRAGON-STAR
LIVES FOREVER (MORE)

A
DRAGON-STAR
LIVES FOREVER (MORE)

J. MICHAEL BROWER

A DRAGON-STAR LIVES FOREVER (MORE)

iUniverse books may be ordered through booksellers or by contacting:

iUniverse
1663 Liberty Drive
Bloomington, IN 47403
www.iuniverse.com
1-800-Authors (1-800-288-4677)

ISBN: 978-1-5320-8623-6 (sc)
ISBN: 978-1-5320-8624-3 (e)

Print information available on the last page.

iUniverse rev. date: 10/28/2019

ACKNOWLEDGEMENT

For John Michael Atnip

All fled, all done
so lift me on the pyre:
The feast is over,
The lamps expire.
—Robert E. Howard, suicide note, 1936

Well deceived are men, the cattle of God
—*Stellar Tombs*, metal band Draconian

I should like to rage through life—this
orthodox creeping is too tame for me
—Jane Wilde

They were lovely and pleasant in their lives and
in their death they were not divided.
—From the gravestone of the Howard family

That book really just kinda wrote itself.
—Ken Kesey, the author of <u>One Flew Over The Cuckoo's Nest</u>

Line from <u>Man of la Mancha</u>, song: *Knight of the Woeful*
Countenance, by Don Mayo; Mary Elizabeth Mastrantonio
and Ernie Sabella, gratefully acknowledged.
(oh, and don't read the footnotes, unless
you <u>really</u> want a dragon ride!)

CONTENTS

CHAPTER ONE

OUR DARKLING SAND

IT IS SAID WE HAVE ABOUT 16 MINUTES.

Someone—or *something*—made a mistake. Let get through what <u>shouldn't</u> have gotten through.

What is it, what's it all mean? It's as if...

This was a man-made error. It was the worst mistake any 'aspiring' civilization could witness.

My female Black World Sword had this to say to me, and telepathically, too:

You have about sixteen minutes, Brian, then your world comes to a whimpering end.

The worst crime possible for humans had been committed.

Missiles, Brian, nuclear missiles just launched from China or North Korea, or somewhere like that, and they are heading for America. As a sword from the Black World, I know when a planet has reached its end, and is well over it. I know, and don't ask me how I know. Should I stop it? I can. You've only got minutes to decide, no pressure.

ICBMs—several ICBMs.

That's Intercontinental Ballistic Missiles, the thing people prefer not to think about. It could change all morality, all sentiment, all the things that make people human. It's the pinnacle of humanitarian crime. The decimation they could make, it would change the world, the long-awaited, post-'dark age.' The worst crime had been committed, and that on the eve of companion departure! This was worse than dragon fire. With dragon fire, things were quick. Nuclear war, people, or forms-of-people, lingered on, radiation their lot.

The missiles were coming from North Korea or China, but that wasn't the point. And 'Armageddon-Now' was coming just before official friendship between the humans and the Crocodilians, and days before all the Alligatorians and the Lizardanians would leave the Earth. Thank God we had dragons to deal with these ICBMs. Not that a dragon-star needs any help when dealing with a missile, mind. It's the greatest error that exists in the world today. This is worse than asteroids-gone-feral. Whether it was just human error or something else, I, Brian Miller, had to deal with it. My sword spoke aloud, probably to get me to move, frozen as I was.

–You've only 16 minutes and you are summoned down to Lincoln Beach, Oregon. By the heir apparent to the Lord of the Lizardanians, Soreidian, no less. You should be overly familiar with his dragon-star-grace, or you ought to be. Sorry for the 'early warning,' but there it is. You're lucky to have Black World swords, monitoring your world and it's many 'misfortunates,' so to speak.

I had a spirited response just barely equal to the occasion.

–Best news I've had today! Can it get any better, just as we are about to leave the Earth? As you know, my precious Black World sword, you just made the spokes come off the wheels.

–I'll just ignore what I don't understand, mimicking you. I think Soreidian made this happen himself!

I looked at the female sword in shock[1].

---

[1] I must say this about my female Black World Sword, just a lil' intro about their total majesty-fantastic. And it's not that I'm bias (yes, I am!). There are about 5,000 'weapons' on the Black World planet. They are located in the Crab Nebula (if you want to know). About 1,000 are Black Swords, 2,000

2

–Let's just collect ourselves.

–This 'collection' has only 15 minutes left, then we'll be in trouble.

–You think that Soreidian, what, programed those missiles to launch?

–Come on Brian, all saurians know that advanced humanity must reach a 'butterfly' planet before it destroys itself. Then God wouldn't have mankind to 'kick around anymore.' For my part, and I'm representing the Black World, I'm for continuing Mankind's suffering. Come on, get ready, do whatever it is that you do! Get a fancy Alligatorian robe on or something formal, just decorate yourself, put on a tie, you'll be on display; come on, hurry up, hurry!

–Wow, just so, my magical sword lady.

I wasn't concerned about Gods' wishes; I was interested in humankind's 'second chance' scenario. Soreidian (that 'mighty dragon') was screwing it all up bigly. Why was he doing this, on his hour of triumph? I wasn't sure if he was just getting back at me for my beating him up trying to save Joan of Arc or getting the better of Danillia during the sparring match on Lizardania. He had it in for me—again! I wasn't in the mood to take this monkey wrench from the Deputy Lord of the Lizardanians and would tell him so.

–I'm not going to do a Harry Potter with you, my noble sword, so—

---

are knives, 1,500 are 'conventional' hatchets or tomahawks, and the rest are 'specialty' weapons, like the three-bladed hatchet that the Warlord of Alligatoria, Larascena, likes to use. I had some 'face-time' with Lara's three-pronged blade during the Twins of Triton adventure. I'm married to Clareina, the Lizardanian, and to Larascena, my female Black World sword just "settled in" with Larascena's male sword, getting married, too. Thing is, 'marriage' means communication, by telepathy and whatever else. All of us live in anarchy, so everyone had absolute freedom, at all times. Communication is everything to a marriage, without it, all is as nothing. Now, my Black World sword has had a lot of injuries, over the years, pieces and parts are not present on her—but she is seasoned, and is the best sword ever, or will ever be, yes, color me totally bias!

—And you won't have to, my viral Clydesdale Noodler Brian! Just look who is coming on strong, your dragons!!!

Of a huge-sudden, Clareina burst into my extensive office. Obviously and completely, my outer workplace was absolutely destroyed by her dragon wings, talons, muscled-moving of the walls themselves, the glass scattering terrifically and every place over my head.

Still, I do like the ladies! My Black sword just barely established an atmosphere over me.

—Sorry about extending my robust power over your fragile laboratory, but this is action-pack! Ah, the dumb swords can clean it all up. You hear what Soreidian is up to, Brian? You've only got 14 minutes, then, BOOM, or so I'm instructed, your world just ends!

My female Black Sword's voice was raised.

—Dumb swords? I'll poke out their massive eyes!

Clareina was looking quite perky and so very excited. She shoved the irate Black World Sword away, good naturedly. Also, she gave no offense for the female Black World sword's criticism. Only between girls; and only a saurian could do this, and the sword reluctantly gave way, to that superior push. I looked Clare up and down, feeling the way any just-married teenager would feel about this fanciful, sexy dragon star[2].

And almost-exactly-then, Larascena came through my shattered window, finishing off what was left of my office, taking it all out in a sinuous cyclone, everything that Clare left behind. It was mostly packed-up, but Lara found a way to be most-destructive. Maybe she heard my voice and was jealous, my talking to Clare before her. Nothing of my office was still standing tall accept me (thanks to my sword's defending atmosphere). My sword was ever watchful of me, even if our leaving was imminent. If I had just this female Black World sword there, everything would be good,

---

[2] Of 'sexy,' just-little-this! The female dragons are the most angelic things, creatures, aliens, any-thing, that I've never, ever seen before and <u>since</u>! Majesty, and sort of regalness, it is so divinely theirs, just talking to a female dragon, you're on your best behavior, just naturally.

I knew she'd give her life to save me. Lara, ignorance covering all her enstrengthened destruction, just looking innocently on, things falling into piles, positively lamenting and crashing down in the talon-ated, elephantine ruin. Of course, all <u>matter</u> itself, was at dragon's-arbitrary-disposal.

At all of this, my sword granted an evil eye to the saurians. Hey, that's hard to do if you're a sword!

–Boy, you do keep this place a mess, Brian. Come on, you Black World weapons, there's clean up in here, what the hell have you been doing-all-the-day? This isn't rocket surgery, you guys, and speaking of, did you hear, Brian? Like humans say, 'Danger's mortal soul is coupled to adventure.' Have you heard what that mischievous Soreidian is up to now? Maybe he's the one responsible for this nuke shit, you think?

At this moment, I had a talk with my sword, knives and hatchets. They knew what to do, and they took off, warp speed.

And at once, even before answering her, I was flying out with Larascena under me. I thought about my words towards Soreidian, out on Lincoln Beach. Maybe I'd take Littorian's approach during the trial we had in Portland, Oregon[3]. By the way, no words can describe the majesty of a flight on a true dragon-star. First, the

---

[3] Just a little from <u>Brian Miller & The Alien Shore</u>, here, and I didn't narrate this myself, so there!

Danillia hadn't changed her wardrobe at all from Vermont. Soreidian looked bitter. To all the humans present, Soreidian looked awesome. A saurian through and through, a Velociraptor with an equine, serious face, his teeth gave him the most notice. The incisors were an incredible six inches long and looked menacing. His long tail looked most dangerous. For this audience, Soreidian didn't care how he looked. Danillia stepped forward getting right up on Brian.

–Well, well! Look at you, Brian Miller, and in these <u>intense</u> days! Nice hair color and the whiteness is on your eyebrows, too! What a Dorian Grey existence; vigorous outside, sickly inside, I'm sure we can thank Littorian for your, uh, miserable appearance. Had a run-in with Death, yes? That's where Littorian will take you, to your (coming) death. I can think of no one who deserves it more! Maybe if you'd read your Bible, you'd know that—

'environment,' they establish around you is really pleasant, no matter

Brian thought he knew how Littorian would take the inveigh. Littorian's eminence was not a factor. Of course, Danillia would go for the human, with all of his faults, which were mounting. Of a sudden, Littorian was no longer in his seat.

Brian looked up to the judge. Judge Greensleeves looked amazingly like Sydney Greenstreet in that instance, and was sitting there open-mouthed, his grey eyes turning away, towards the wall.

Brian just had time to see Danillia sailing away. Littorian punched her. He could have ripped her head off, and then some. Lightening quick, he gave her a tremendous punch across the jaw, and she crumbled like a doll into the wall, twenty feet away. He could have taken the jaw off, but there were humans around. The wall, made of marble, crumbled too, but managed to stay together.

The judge, belatedly, seeing the 'innocent' woman thrown across the room, banged his gavel. Judge Greensleeves shucked his jowls relentlessly.

—Sir, you're out of order. Restrain yourself!

Littorian stiffened, almost regretting his salami tactics, and then sat down.

—Yes, your honor.

Of course, it would have finished off a human, leaving quite a significant splat. But Danillia rose, rather awkwardly. She wiped off her green suit. Then, without a word, Danillia just matter-of-factly took a seat at the prosecutor's table. She gave a little huff and looked at the ceiling, crossed-legged. The little ribbon in her hair, she set right again.

Soreidian, looking on at the spectacle, leaned across to Littorian, his abdominals riding like iron bubble rap on the desk.

—You're going to pay with your life for that. You too, Brian Miller human!

Brian put on his McKayla Maroney smirk at Soreidian's mean countenance.

—Quit your silly catastrophizing. My tinfoil-hat be strong, what a continuous mockery you are, Soreidian. Just sit your titsicles down; your whack-off light is now dimmed toad-man, so cease your word-vomiting.

Soreidian just stared at Brian incredibly, because Brian made his announcement in Universalian, and his stroke didn't interfere with his dirty words inventory. Soreidian totally resented the 'inclination' to call him a snake-man, or a lizard-man, or any kind of worm or creepy-crawling thingy-thing existing in the lexicon of humankind.

how fast they are flying, with just a little wind blowing at you, for effect only. The dragons can't take you 'as fast' as, say, Tiperia, that

---

–I'll take care of you personally, Brian Miller. I'll mush that injured brain right up. You're so pasty and abrasive you'll look just like toothpaste in my clamping jaws.

–I'm looking forward to our toothpaste-date, and I'll be sure to bring my light sabre. Just get back to your hole, you simpering, fish-eyed bureaucrat. You've got a learning curve as flat as Kansas, just call me up if you want gangster, you blinkered frog-man.

Soreidian twisted with rage. To be insulted by a human! Brian would be reduced to dust before his lips closed, anywhere else.

Littorian then spoke at a little whisper, secretly enjoying his companion's mockery of Soreidian.

–Now, why don't you take a seat, Soreidian? Or you'll end up the same way as Danillia. That'll cause us a scene. Wouldn't want that, right, my Lord of the Lizardanians?

–This trial will determine that! I didn't want to take your place, but I've no choice now.

–We are venturing on new times, then, you and me. I'm innocent, you know that—my innocence just had a way with me, back there.

–You've pushed things too far. And now, this Companion Program is in ruins! The only companions left are in this room, right here! Is that the form of 'leadership,' you've got in mind? You aren't deserving of the power you've got! No one should have approved the Companion Program!

–This trial will determine all of that, also. Now, let's begin. We haven't got all day, you know. I use to call you friend. I see that's been antiquated.

Soreidian narrowed the distance between himself and Littorian.

–You're out of control.

–I'm just getting started! Just keep your shirt on. Whoops, you're naked, just didn't notice that!

–At least we're in agreement about leaving Earth.

–We are, at least you're stupidvising is loosely working to some extent. Good boy!

Soreidian ground his sizeable teeth in response. Then, Soreidian just sighed. He went back to the prosecutor's desk. He didn't like those juvenile expressions from Littorian at all. Danillia, totally recovered, but put-out and slighted, slid over some papers. Soreidian snatched up the pages and began reading to the court.

demi-god, but almost that fast. Second, on their mighty shoulders, muscled wings 60 feet on either side of you, merrily defying gravity like it was an unruly, errant child, reaching for what you <u>can be</u>, leaving <u>what you are</u> wailing in the dust behind you. The third is just-this: The incredible comfort, the <u>feel</u> of their warm scales, muscled skin about your legs as you ride, nothing can be so fantastic, nothing could be so important, vital, it's even essential, registered as a part of life itself. These three features are a golden ring of fire that no sincere companion can ever out-do, opiates be (God) damned.

–Yes, I've heard, times two or three. Lara, should I be a little obsequious to Soreidian, if he is—

Larascena, as usual, read my mind.

–No, I don't think you need to suck-up to him at all. Incidentally, Brian, what is the half-life of a lie? Can't you see that time makes things, sometimes, the truth later on? All things are in flux, even if you don't see it. The Earth was flat, that was the truth. Now, we see that was a lie. And what of its shape eons from now? We judge lies currently, immediately, here, now. What a lie will become, well, who knows? Maybe a lie is just a newborn truth. And it can wrap itself up through time. A lie, the truth, a lie again. Thesis, Antithesis, Synthesis. And it's all related to time. As a human, with a limited life span, you can't see that a lie, is the truth, and is a lie again, much later on, and with improvement to yourself! Can a Cro-Magnon man operate an Apple Computer or launch a nuclear missile? Today, mankind has and can! Oh, that Soreidian is being such a dirt-bag right now and just as we were about to leave? If your taught wrong, then that's your truth—for humans, it all depends on the time you are taught—truth is very volatile. What's he thinking? I'm going to get in his muzzle.

–Now, Lara, maybe we can be a little diplomatic?

Clareina, overhearing our talk even while in extreme flight, had this to say:

–Not before I get in his pig-pen face with my avenging claws, and I'd appreciate your non-interference, my dual-husband, lest I spank you severely. You may dissent without prejudice from me, Brian, but you're behind I will own. You approve, Lara?

—Oh, you bet, I'll take one half-moon, you the other, okay, Clare?

CHAPTER TWO

HIGH DRAGON DUNGEON

I WAS COMFORTED WITH PROTECTIONS, MY TWO PISTOLS PROVIDED by Kerok, my Black World weapons, and my many-dragon-stars. My dragon lowered herself to the sand.

Soreidian just stamped on the missile under his commanding monster boot, denting the forlorn rocket in half-way. I couldn't tell if it was a Russian missile, from North Korea or if it was from China. It didn't matter, this 'thing' could change humanitarian history. Since it was under his commandeering foot, I assumed it was inert.

Amazingly, just as we were about to have our polemical outrage, the North Korean 'skinny kid,' Ji-hun Kim showed up. Thing was, he wasn't 'skinny' anymore: He was buff, at least 140 nimble pounds, and used his Lizardanian training to get well ahead of me on Lincoln Beach. Kim bounded off his female Alligatorian dragon-star when she was 20 feet in the air, running up to Soreidian and bowed almost to the ground.

–My lord, I'm so, so sorry! I think my country bears responsibility for this and I'm—

Soreidian's voice was raised.

−Begone, you stupid human! I'm interested in the companion to the Lord of the Lizardanians, this is no place for you!

−My good lord, so please you, but this missile is one that—

−Gods, damn this mankind beast! I'm not interested in your silly excuses, you vermin pile! Get gone to your silly dragon and just let me get at Brian Miller.

At that, without a word, the Alligatorian dragon snapped her claws together, and Kim dutifully went to her side. I stopped him on his shameful walk to his reptilian.

−Hey, don't worry. I think Soreidian programmed these missiles himself. We have Black World weapons going to the Americans, explaining all, so there will be no retaliation. Just let me handle it and perk up.

−Thank you, Brian, I'm so glad to be a companion, we were at— Soreidian's booming voice drown out Kim big-time.

−What was left unfinished 65 million years ago will be finished now. Sorry to task-rabbit you, but I think you know how serious this is. Oh, Oregon; I always get massive wood here? Get it, Brian? Don't get your squeezums in a bundle. So, I'm glad to see you here, Brian, and just in time, too. Come on, now, that's the way, just let that meaningless companion be. Danillia and I were just discussing families, then I saw you out on the horizon, just flying with your own fickle 'family.' You humans seek to torture each other by getting your families involved. Even Sherlock Holmes and Moriarty get the 'relatives' boiled into their little nonsense, for instance, when Doctor Watson (I presume), in <u>A Game of Shadows</u>, was threatened. All of you go after the families for reprisal, a punishment for you personally, since you feel for them. This is definitely not in our saurian connection or culture (if there is one, because I'm dealing with simple-you, we'll <u>suppose</u> there is), it smacks anarchy (or autarky, whatever) in the face. If we have a problem with you, it's you alone that is 'accountable.' Do you recall that movie, I mentioned?

−No, my lord.

–But you did see <u>A Game of Shadows</u>?

–My lord, it was one of the movies I entertained Littorian with, and I think he was soon asleep, as was usual, and—

–So, you didn't see the book that Holmes gave to Moriarty to get "an inscription" on?

–My good and gracious sir, your—

–The book was <u>The Dynamics of an Asteroid & Lecture Notes</u>?

–Are you asking me or telling me, my lord?

Soreidian just dismissed (and despised) my civility with a clawed waive.

–And that is the whole subject of why we are still here in the first place, the asteroid collision with your silly, game-playing planet. You are going into the Darkest Days, the post-nuclear war times, when morality, or any kind of happiness is out the blighted window. For you, I'm standing on the 'phallic' symbol, the nuke, that can bring these darkling years. I thought everything would be over very quickly, yet, here you are plaguing us like a virus and—

–Oh, I see, my family is excluded? This is something new and—

–Anyway, the families we don't involve, when we have an issue with you. Every human pet has a story. It is another distinguishment we have from your vile race. Don't you see? For instance, your Karl Marx was a total popper! If he'd been supported and better-off, then he'd be a genius, then and now! Now he's a genius, but then, in London where he lived, was he a genius? He didn't get English citizenship, you know. Look at the letter he wrote to Engels saying <u>Das Kapital</u> had been published. He thanks Engels for sending him money! The one percent have nothing to justify their position, so they need war, they want a war, with you, physio-pseudo-revolutions and workers leading it all! You see, you have a limited life span! It's war within your bodies all the time, and peace without? Oh, please. That's the reason why you don't have peace reigning all the time. Viruses, strains, pandemics, just the 'common' cold, that's why it's war, war all the time! Thing is, you have all these nukes running around. Blowing up the rich and poor alike? Can't have that! Let's talk about Apocalypse Now, and it won't take long. Kill the women, the children and the men—kill them all with nukes, that's war. You're DNA is equal to your born-in-malice. And cleaning up isn't changing your maladroit DNA. So, your elite is scared of war now. That's the only thing keeping 'your people' alive: Thank God, or Allah, for the Muslims, something to get your industrial-military complex on. The science of absolute destruction! I think saurians shouldn't interfere with that decision. You are the loose screw in that whole affair, and I'm not talking about your wives. If you know only the 'classic' literature, and that is fine, you will always number among the bourgeoisie. Maybe that will do, for you, but you will never be a 'real' revolutionary. And you think of yourself as a revolutionary, right, Brian? You are, at best, a chandelier rebel with a dragon-star cause, not a human one. Your so deceived about this, it's really comical. Dragon-stars think nothing is inevitable, and just maybe nothing is. Your 99% needs distraction; they want distraction; they crave distraction! Your one, two or five percent needs non-nuclear-war, capitalism, the grotesque, oppressive, nightmare-state, the opiate industry, modeled media that they can control. But if it's nuclear war, the elite will be infected by the radiation, too. No one 'having' nukes ever 'gave' them up. Oh, I guess Brazil and Argentina did with this Treaty of Tlatelolco in 1967, but the more militant countries don't. Humanity is a nuke-accident-that-has-already-happened. I mean, look at Chernobyl, Fukushima and whatever else you have been covering up? I really resent Teresian, the Wysterian, and now Kerok, getting rid of all that radiation! Humanity quite deserves a couple of thousand rads, rems, sieverts, becquerels, and (wormwood) grays! You need dragons, dragons surely don't need you. It's like when Moriarty lost that game of chess to Holmes, you alone are responsible for—

I interrupted Soreidian. I virtually had to scream he was being so loud.

–Hey, it's too bad Moriarty wasn't that great a chess player. We all knew how that movie would end, my lord.

—But do you! Do you know how this movie, this situation, will end <u>for you</u>? You will be held accountable for the actions (or inactions) that you perform in this lifetime. Tiperia should have let those two asteroids destroy this planet and I don't give a care if she started it or not. You're just whispering past the graveyard, Brian. You will all die by a limited nuclear war anyway, but now the Crocodilians are here, maybe preventing that! You can't have a so-called "LNA" Limited Nuclear Attack, it'd go viral (or I'll see that it <u>does</u> go viral). You're 'overall morality' will be sustained by them, you have 'tamed' them into protecting you. Are you proud of yourself? Contemptable, abhorrent, disgusting things you are! Your fate is brutality but now you use Crocodilians to protect you from your-own-fool-selves. You've lost Lizardanians and Alligatorians but gained our arch-enemy Crocodilians for your protection! Or are you, indeed, like every other writer out there just 'looking for an honorable way out'? Is that your epitaph? I'd go the way of Robert E. Howard if I were you and this, friend Brian, is (really) wormwood.

—Let's pull back a second, my lord and—

—No! Let's leave it inserted, impaled, filled-up, pierced, skewered and bigly speared! Isn't that what you're doing to two saurians these days? It's an obscenity, your copulating with these eminent reptilians. I don't know what you call the euphoria of the sexual act, normally it's over in a minute or two. Now it lasts about six or seven minutes, right? The magic of dragon-stars has you going to great heights. It's disgusting from <u>our</u> end not from yours! You're just a—

—A giant size Olympian Pacharan, my lord, yes, I'm the dragon-induced-magic-teenager! Sure, let's leave it plunged-to-the-massive-sacks-in, and why not? Thank you, my lord and next time (which follows hard upon, because my saurian women are looking antsy just now), I'll think of you, especially as I climax (which is very often). I'm getting excited getting back to my disbursement schedule, and are we done?

—Calm your bowling ball bags for now, you wanna-be stud, and listen to me. Humanity is on the line now, not <u>your</u> pitiful stones.

When will you think that God just <u>isn't</u>? When will you not believe in anything? You know that time is coming. You really know how to bring it out of a saurian don't you my skinny fuck?

–Words like those, my lord, wow, you're getting down to your bitch-ass wormy nature, I'm truly blessed. I wouldn't like to see you turned loose on Skid Row in Los Angeles. You'd find plenty of the human walking-dead there. Everyone in the Skids has a hidden agenda. You, Soreidian, would pile up the bodies after those kinds of insults if someone down there had said them, probably burn up all 50,000 homeless (or more). You'd have to use magic, the fire in you <u>*just isn't*</u>.

–I know what you're talking about, don't think I don't, Brian. Skid Row, that is just the place for all humanity. Most of those people want to be there, on Skid Row, they are like in that movie the Matrix, and would vote that people <u>don't want</u> to be awake, but real life (capitalism, socialism, communism) is too hard on them. They want to be high! Hell, the Nordic countries understand this, and more. Anyway, Brian, you'll get worse than Skid Row, anon, you incredibly dopey, hallow eyed sticky teenager. As you know, existence for humans is a kind of punishment. Your bodies, internally, writhe with the same things, rich or poor, everyone suffers. You war within these same-self bodies, hence your war-ing outside as well.

–Wow, I thought it was all our phallic symbolism, this warring, like what your standing on right now, a friendly missile. I don't take things for granted; I know I'm lucky. I guess all revolutions end under your talons, my lord?

–Ah, revolutions! Even your Trotsky (not his real name) has his faults—marriage and his polyandries, questionable family life, and still you hope for that Helphand-Parvus-inspired "permanent revolution." Helphand's actual name was Israel Lazarevich Gelfand, talk about your Jewishness! Racist? Sign me up for that! I'm not into getting into the miniscule historical cracks, and into your foolish, pharaonic history, and I might have it all wrong, but I really don't think so, I'm sorry to be so down-right "bougie" about a primitive thing like your history. All this revolution, your 'Robin Hoodism,' that 'steals from the rich to give to the poor,' all leads to silly authoritarianism not anarchism-of-the-saurian-kind. You humans cannot achieve such; your welcome to try, it's so entertaining to see humanity trip over its own shoelaces. There is the fashion it should be in, but this is the way things really are. It's a human's problem, and you sort it, right? Evil in good? War within, peace without? Convicted of the deceit of humankind, I'm not trying to convert you to my view, little Simian. All humans are such contradictions. Just look at these 'advanced' humans, Andrew Joseph Stack III (ramming a plane into the Internal Revenue Service building) or Theodore John Kaczynski (your Unabomber, mailing death). Geniuses or psychos, you'll be the judge, not I. They elected violence, not debate, an indictment of man. And after the first nukes you'll know that you are just animals, as your brains are reduced to walnut size after the radiation strikes your people. I'm not talking about all the drugs, and alcohol you use because you can't face 'real life,' and all the literature out there like the Turner Diaries, Mein Kampf, and all that silly Satanist shit. DNA determines all, don't you get that? You think you can take a Dzhokhar Tsarnaev or a Joseph Stalin and 'raise them here' and not have DNA determining all? You can influence 'hearts and minds' but if they are 'listening' to their DNA, and like a drug, and Skid Row, what honest human can't? Not to listen to your DNA is the exception. All of this is just a human-kind-race to get off your planet into the butterfly or goldilocks zone. I can't believe that Teresian is doing this, but she's getting you five or seven planets to 'mess up,' just like you've done to Earth. That's your secret on escaping 'Climate Change,' here. You, Brian Miller Human, have elected saurians to do this, to save you. I resist. In your schools, you have to learn and then conform. Never really think. You see that really thinking isn't really conforming. So, you are marginalized. Like Rene Descartes said, doubt of everything. By the way, he didn't 'say' it first, he's just given the 'credit.' Thing is, if people do like the 'star-dragon story,' they will just steal it from you or anybody. Be prepared! Remember, the happy accident of your birth shouldn't determine the outcome of your life.

–What you <u>learn</u> in talking to you, my gracious lord. I'm in Soreidian school? What a fat hypocrite you are. I think you've been using the same mouthwash as Danillia, my lord, your breath smells like you've been sucking android-dragon-monster-cock, it has that chewed toenail stench that I <u>and your whore mother</u> have warned you about. Just talking to you is like being in dragon prison, you epic worm.

Then Soreidian hissed, flexing his iron, airplane-'n'-tank-'n'-building crushing jaws. I just didn't care about his stupid plans. I wish I did. The Black World weapons and all my saurians were at sixes-and-sevens, fearing how much danger I was in.

–I could squash and squish your body into a golf ball in a micro-second, human-rat-scum! Thank goodness you have some dragon blood in there, I think some of you might be tasty. Oh, if you didn't have your Black World Sword just sitting there, floating there, smirking at me, you'd be in a forgotten grave! Come here Brian, I'll make your body into a thimble just to show Larascena who is the human-berserker-boss, aside from your blood, which, for clean-up, I'll consume!

This last made Larascena growl and it was striking, at least to me. She wanted to kill Soreidian, and it wasn't the first time, either.

I knew I was ripping Soreidian up and, just like Mike Tyson said, everyone's got a plan until they get punched in the face. Soreidian was the most mercurial saurian I'd ever met. He'd be cool one minute, building-shattering the next. To have his awesome power 'unchecked' was just another reason to have the Lizardanians and the Alligatorians off this planet, and back benignly terrorizing all the galaxies humanity had yet to explore.

I had some intense teenage concerns, too. The loin ripping notions about my wives and getting back to their enjoys and niceties as they stretched and manipulated my kick balls around in those giant, enstrengthened, sinuous, sensuous hands-'n'-claws.

Oh, I couldn't wait for some 'alone time' with the two of them. To think my saurian wives could earthquake *whole nations* with those extraordinary hands, and yet be so, so gentle and soothing; damn, you couldn't go no better. It was a loving intensity outshining all the hardest drugs. A night with a female saurian is just ineffable, opiates be damned. I'm not a homosexual, but a night with a <u>male</u> saurian would be just as ineffable. Not that there is anything wrong with being homosexual, I respect that proclivity. I had no truck in debating with Soreidian, he had his rascal mind made up in advance, all my speechifying he just dismissed outright. The only reason he was being grudgingly reasonable, was the company I kept.

Danillia had shown up and let Jason Shireman and Rachel Dreadnought solemnly down. The two stoic companions stood on Lincoln beach, near enough to Danillia to be hit with a sabre. Danillia would have stomped me into the ground until I was no more, I knew her mind so very well. She hated me always, like when I first saw her, shapeshifted or otherwise. Overall, I wish I could establish a peace between every one of us, but the initial hatred of Soreidian and Danillia continued on, even when Danillia was shape-shifted into Leah Starblue. The incident when I ran into her on Lizardania with Korillia was probably burning hot-and-heavy in her rascally mind. In that incident, she defeated Korillia, but was dealt a crushing blow by the Wysterian Kukulkan. And again, that was because I was calling out to any and every saurian to be of assistance to Korillia.

Danillia had a very satisfied look, then telepathed to me.

You'll get yours, Terran. Oh, yes, and it will be more pain than I could give by ripping out your organs. You humans are bored-for-war, just look at that missile 'under a certain saurian's foot,' hinting of Genesis right now? Oh, you're too dumb to see it. Go on and live this charade, you simian-nosed, thingy-thing. It will be so good to be rid of you. Brian Miller, you have a strange need to be lifted up, and bone-crushed by a saurian; we'll see to that soon enough. Let's draconianly endeavor to privatize your pain into a little, bloody pile of crimson rags, capitalizing on the fear your having now. We need to leave planet Earth, and that's why you can't have nice things, and, besides, you are just getting in the way.

Interestingly to me, Rachel and Jason just looked sad! They both looked down into the sand, like they were looking for a diamond, or some-such. I'd never seen them like this before. Obviously and completely, they were in on the plan 'hatched' by Soreidian and Danillia.

I looked back at my awesome, tower of reptilian back-up. And I've never seen a collection of saurians so spunky and mean-looking, just behind me. Littorian the Lord of the Lizardanians was my companion and I winked at him. I remembered the haughty way he'd talked to Soreidian before. Littorian, though, stared nervously at Soreidian, maybe expecting something bad. Larascena, Warlord of Alligatoria, and Clareina were bulked up and looking really hostile, and just then even Kukulkan, the greatest, strongest Wysterian ever known was there, and Korillia the virtual Warlord of Lizardania, too! They must have arrived from Lizardania. My Black World weapons were poised to intervene very quickly if Soreidian grew surly. His disguise was Soreidian's own, I had no idea (as per usual with me). My two Kerok-inspired guns, Right and Left Two Hands could fire instantly.[4] They both checked their loads as if they were famous

---

[4] Just a word about the pistols, from Book III, the guns are so funny!

–I have a gift to bring before Brian Miller. Stop with the drum roll, please.

Kerok produced a large box.

Brian opened it.

Inside were two handguns.

–These are guns for your two hands, Brian Miller. When not holding weapons from the Black World, right? As a pair, they are "Two Hands," and they are sisters. On their own, there's Right and Left. The larger one is Left, and she's pretty feisty. The smaller one, her kid-sister is very conservative for

porn stars, making doubly sure all cylinders were full and potent.

---

a pistol. And you'd want to be <u>conservative</u> with so little ammunition, right? Formally, I'm introducing you to Right Two Hands, and Left Two Hands. Now you know the full panoply. I won't tell you the trouble I went to on any of this.

Brian had a tendency to snicker. He just couldn't contain himself and thought this was pretty hilarious. Kerok wasn't laughing. Kerok eyed them in the box and Brian in a very critical way.

—There, you see? They even have three names, just like you, Brian Miller. What's your middle name?

—I'm afraid I don't have one.

—What? You don't? I thought that was common in all American names, not like British or French with four, five or six names? I'm misinformed about my studies of your culture?

—No, my lord, you've got it right. I wasn't given one, it's just Brian Miller. It's just, well, Brian Miller.

—Difficult child this, but no matter. I won't be dissuaded from giving you this gift. They will protect you, insurance for the Black Weapons. I hope they see it so; they can work together, if diplomatically arranged. Well, they <u>have</u> three names; I was just trying to relate them to something familiar, so that's a fail.

—Sorry my lord, I'm just a burberry ape, right now.

—With the adventures all set up for you, I think it's time you had something familiar, something like pistols. Kind of reminds you of <u>Treasure Island</u>, right? Though they can introduce themselves, when the time is right, the Left holds nine rounds, and Right has three rounds. I've given you three sets of rounds for each gun, as seen on the left, just there. Come back to me if you need more, they are extremely difficult to manufacture. Even someone so incredible as a saurian would be very surprised by the power of each gun. By the way, the bullets are not alive, but the guns are. If you're facing a saurian, the bullets won't penetrate them, but it will knock them down and that soundly. They'll be very frustrated when they get up again and you'd better have your Black sword with you facing an irate saurian. If you get them in the face, the rounds will taste a little salty to them, and it is repugnant, which the guns will like. Obviously, when facing a saurian, rely on your Black Weapons.

Brian's Black Weapons, very surprised at the gift, looked furtively in the box, now open on the dining room table. The Black sword just did a 'harrumph,' and then backed out away from the box, her nose in the air, as much as a sword can demonstrate such an action. She tried desperately to be respectful to Kerok, knowing what everyone felt about him.

–It's nice of you to so equip our young companion here, Kerok, but it's hardly necessary.

–You might be over your head, on some occasion, then, it'd be nice to have some back-up.

–Me? I'm trying to be a companion to this human, here, not a confidant.

Brian tucked the Black female sword in, backing her up, coyly nuzzling her now.

–Hey, why don't you see your man, floating over by Larascena now? I think he wants a session with you.

–Really? Rut-row; I'm not even ready. Are you sure?

–It's okay, I'm very well protected, just go, I'm okay.

Larascena's sword, as if on cue hearing his 'name,' floated away from his master and cocked his hilt and guard slightly, nodding to Brian.

–Are you sure, Brian?

–Oh yeah.

–Think to me if there is any trouble. Especially from those laughable pop-guns.

At that, Brian heard a noise coming from inside the box! It sounded like a sucking of teeth, but Brian couldn't be sure.

–Have a good time, wheeling around your little potato shooters.

The two pre-married Black Swords departed. The other weapons went with them. Brian tried to address Kerok in a timorous way.

–Thank you Kerok, for this generous gift, I hope I won't need them.

–As sure as there are stars hanging brightly in the sky, you'll need them.

Brian then shut his mouth and gawked at Kerok. Kerok pressed the point and nodded his reptilian head up and down.

–Am I gonna need these guns?

–You might. Instructions are just there. I don't 'see,' the future but I can feel it.

–Thank you, Kerok you're the supreme, the utmost strongest—

–Unctuousness for me? Save that for Larascena, if you're going to marry her. And Clareina, too. You're going to marry a Lizardanian and our Warlord? Damn, you're gonna have your hands full and a half. I've a secret I'll just share with you now, Brian, something to ruminate on later (or all your life). You think there is nothing after you die, right? No heaven, hell, purgatory, no limbo, et cetera? Listen to this, it's important. Nothing happens until the

End of Time. When you die, really die, you get there, well, just like that! At Time's End, everything is reborn and it happens just like that, only a moment of pain, see? No, you don't see. Everything that's EVER been is reborn at Time's End. There is something you can look forward to seeing.

–Right, right, my lord. Is there enough room for them?

–Room? How big is the universe, my friend? The universe goes on forever. Oh, I think there is just enough room.

–I see.

–No, no you don't.

–I don't see.

–Never mind Brian. Try to think about it—if you die by violence, fear not, you'll be reborn at Time's End, in the next second. At Time's End, everything and everyone, reborn! Don't you see?

Brian didn't want to be disrespectful to Kerok, then. He didn't say that Time with Death Incarnate could be an eternity. Brian then looked at the directions rolled up on the surface of the oak box. Brian couldn't believe that all of this wasn't a joke.

TAKE

FIRE

AIM (if you want to)

REPEAT

DONE

Brian suddenly laughed. Kerok's permanent lines, didn't increase in the slightest.

–I think I'll commit this to memory.

Kerok did the traditional shaking of the head, drawing it back.

–Uh-huh, well, we'll talk later, okay, Brian? You'd better introduce yourself; I'll cease my advice right there.

Instantly, Kerok left. Brian took the gift box into a little anteroom. It was sparsely populated by one desk, one chair, and one light. Tiperia invented it, but it wasn't to be used. It would do for Brian.

–Hi, I'm Brian Miller, pleased to meet you, my noble pistols!

The guns rose, out of their places, and looked around. They did it with barrel pointed downwards, just to be cordial. One was a large handgun, and it looked massive, too big to hold on to. It looked roughly like a .357, but had three barrels. It was capable of firing nine shots, three at a time, if necessary.

Brian looked down at the case and saw three sets of cartridges. The other was smaller and looked like a large derringer. It also had a three-shot barrel. It too had three sets of cartridges. Brian did some quick math. There were twenty-seven shots in the first gun, nine in the second, totaling 36. Brian thought about the numbers and then wondered if they were already loaded.

Brian's sword and other weapons then burst into the room. Brian's female Black sword didn't want to spend that much time with 'her man,' anyway. The guns turned to the Black World weapons, but had their barrels still pointed down.

–And who the fuck am you?

–Now, now, it's alright. I'm just getting acquainted with our new friends, okay? The pistols obviously have gutter mouths; I'm sure, no offense, all around, right?

Left Two Hands spoke right up.

–I'll verbally adjust. Who this is?

The Black sword just wrapped her guard into a bagel-mouth. Left Two Hands took advantage.

–Yup, new friends. That means sayonara to old friends, y'all get that? Don't you askhole's get it? Don't let the door hit you in the ass, right, my lil' fork 'n' spoons, get that? Wow, she looks like she's goin' to shoot a deuce, right now.

Brian's sword responded angrily.

–No, we don't 'get that.' I've difficulty answering because your question is screwed up.

–Well aren't you just a fart in a dish pan, then, isn't that right, kid-sister? How about getting this cock-o'-sucker!

At that, Left Two Hands cocked herself, pointing at the Black sword. Before Brian could say anything, even getting in the way of the barrel, the hammer came down.

–BANG! We fuckers don't die so easily, especially to rock-tumbler brain, piece-o-shit chop sticks like you! You're so up your own ass, I just laugh at your shit. Damn, you just got poonaged!

Of course, nothing came out, the hammer just clicked down, and the kid-sister laughed and laughed. The Black sword did a little jump, the hammer was so loud. It was very funny to see the little Right Two Hands acting comic. The hatchet and the knives were more than irate. Brian's sword was livid.

–Did you see what she did?!

The senior gun mimicked Brian's Black sword, at a perfect pitch!

Everyone, only twenty yards away, action-pack-ready. Now satisfied, both Right and Left Two Hands, had their hammers pulled back, aimed at Soreidian's head. They also had two Black World knives threatening to bring Armageddon booming out, just chattering away at the triggers, waiting word to fire. Left Two Hands, spoke up.

Now we have someone to pull our triggers, Brian. Remember on Crocodilia? We couldn't pull our own triggers just when we were loaded. Now, that's corrected thanks to your own willing Black World knives.

Right Two Hands also mentally spoke to me.

Don't question me about my 'small arms,' I'm ready for action-pack(age), I'm ready to send the best bullets I have to his cranium, I think the ears are the vulnerable place, I'm just waiting for the word!

–Did you see what she did? Yo, go toss my salad, mean bitch! What a blue-haired, drop-kicked, saffle lady we have here, this Devil's joystick is kinda quick, kid-sister, so watch out! This sword has got the bark of an old biddy in a wheelchair.

The Black sword swung at Left Two Hands—and definitely missed! The gun was much faster than it appeared.

–Well, hidden nigglette—did you see what that cod smasher did? That big-bird bitch, she's a number six, shit, she's pissed, best watch out, kid-sister. Hey, human, why don't you ditch this wild boar, this old burnt cookie, and select a real woman to go out with? That nigger sword is a winy bitch. You don't wanna listen to her foolish slag heap innuendo, do you? You never know when she's on the rag, that fun-sucker, definitely irregular.

–I'm not a fan-of-you. You asked for this, hopeless ho; outside, Left Two Hands, you and me, and throw in your kid-sister just for tears.

Brian then intervened, pushing the wild Black sword out of the way of Left Two Hands. She just missed cutting Brian to pieces. She was well aware of this, limiting her strikes, given the situation on Manitou, what Brian liked to call their "Nuclear World". She didn't and couldn't cut Brian again, and the Black Sword staggered back.

–We can settle all of this later. I'll just have to have a word with Kerok.

At that, Brian left, tucking the guns into his belt. Untouchable by the female Black sword, Left Two Hands sucked her teeth and gibed at the sword, snickering all the while, now safely "tucked in" to Brian's belt.

Soreidian turned, now jerking my head around, stopping my mental communications.

–You want to defend humanity. You don't have the power to defend it. To defend humanity, is dress rehearsal to destroy it. That's Nature's Way. A limited nuclear war wouldn't be 'limited.' You don't see any of this. Look at <u>Castle Keep</u>, by William Eastman, for example. Yes, I've frequented your library. There is a quote by Captain Beckman on page 237, "But I still don't think we should defend, destroy the castle." Are you familiar with this book?

–I know I have it, I've read it in parts.

–You haven't followed through reading it completely, typical of you.

–Yes, your grace.

I decided to be civil again, just so I could figure out where he was going with his questioning.

–You want humanity to live on.

–Obviously, that. But I want more than that, my regent.

–You're afraid of me, human?

–What <u>human</u> wouldn't be my lord?

–Answering questions with questions, cheeky, cheeky. You want all humanity to become dragons, live forever, and explore more than Teresian's Butterfly zone?

My sarcasm came back. And I screamed out my response, and I just didn't care about being unctuous, right then.

–I know my secret is safe with you, my dick lord. I don't know where you've been, but we established peace between all saurians, everywhere. Eons, millenniums worth of war ended. The humans had something to do with that, and I did more than my share. That alone should guarantee our defense against ourselves through the Crocodilians, with no interference from you. Didn't you yourself announce a peace between all saurians everywhen, any place and everywhere? You are free to go (so go), I mean, goddamn, I'm so done with you, fucking really, you are like Littorian once said: Silly saurian, you are a real tin-foil hat wearing space cadet.

Soreidian was really furious at my lack of genuflection. He did advance on me, but slowly, slowly.

–You are as devious as a wormy-snake. Recall, power isn't taught, it's there naturally. Now you are proposing to change your overall governing (a shitty term for a devout anarchist to use) from a global oligarchic elite to a companion-dominated dictatorship via these groveling, toady Crocodilians! You're so stupid, I can smell the dumb on you, your little 'dream' about the Crocodilians destroying Earth just might come true. Oh, yes, I'm aware of that little dream, and it is your worst nightmare. Just look at your jubilee and juvenile government in this country, you owe 20 trillion dollars? Why can't it be 22 trillion, 25, 30, 60 or 165 trillion? You can't pay that back—so revolution is your fate eventually. Maybe your clingers, deplorables, crazy lunatics, and irredeemables will turn about and advance your communist bromides. And that revolution will have a conservative reaction which has always been the case. Then, post-revolution, you can wipe it all out like a school blackboard and start over again with debt: Like Alexander Hamilton says the greater the debt, the greater the credit. And Alexander—

My voice, raised.

–Yeah and look how Hamilton ended up: Shot by Burr!

–You're going to destroy all the saurian's worlds, just in defending humanity, you are like Major Falconer in Castle Keep! I'll get to the end of this sentence if it obliterates you. But obliterates you slowly, oh so slowly, like the rise of a great captain, and his fall into this capitalist muck, just like the castle falling to the Nazis around Falconer. I think all humanity gets to a point where you just want an honorable way out. An intelligent surfer swims along with the waves, yes? Just like a dead man would. You'll destroy the irreplaceable castle to 'keep' people free? You're a fool. You're a chandelier communist and a Champaign socialist, and you've said that yourself! You thought you were being self-critical, but it's more than that. You're sustaining a revolution that's evaporating in a bureaucratic nightmare, that's what is happening with those Crocodilians coming here, dealing with these vial humans. You confuse style with substance, you think you can just 'smooth' through everything. This planet is a piece of shit. I'm not for telling you anything, I'm for <u>showing</u> you!

With that, faster than any other saurian or Black World weapon could even perceive, Soreidian touched my forehead. Some, I'm sure, had their scaly-not-brows go appreciably up in surprise, but none had time for physical action. Of a sudden, no <u>time</u> existed.

Dream.

It was just.

It was just a dream.

An extensive, far-reaching, extraordinarily conceived, and, in sections, a titillating dream. The waves, once roaring, were languid, grave-keeper-calm. Everything and everywhere, orange. I looked from West to East. Beach oaks and Evergreens were a complete architecture of Godzilla gone bat-fire crazy. Every tree, ripped by the roots, thrown hither and thither about like toys in a baby's sinister playpen. And then, I saw them.

CHAPTER SUB-ONE

APOCALYPSE HERE

No DRAGON-STARS. No-STAR-DRAGONS. No STARS.
No Black World weapons.
No companions.
No dragons.
He's been yanked out of here; he's been taken away.
And no life at all.
Except <u>sea lions</u>.

I had no memory. Just a few things. My dragons, I had such feelings for them. They came back first. The memory was a bit misty and feint. I looked up and down the seacoast.

My mind, confused. Everything was veiled in orange or some version of sickly carrot-color.

I was on a beach, the same beach, Lincoln Beach. The mushroom explosions in the sky, now fading away, but you could still see them. They blanketed the Western side of America everything and everywhere, orange.

On the beach, crawling to the strange waves, were sea lions maybe a dozen of them. And then when I looked out to the skyline, a dozen more, bobbing in the sickly waves. My robes were gone, replaced by short cargo pants, half-way to my foot, and a green short sleeved shirt with two breast pockets. My legs were turned to liquid bags, and I wobbled. It was just like experiencing my stroke all over again: My mind was completely shocked by my stroke, I was data-throating myself, trying to remember. I had beaten tennis shoes on, the high-top kind. Of the shoes, I hadn't worn them in years (well, last year). I didn't feel weird, irritated, I just felt, I don't know, forgotten.

Then a voice!

–Help me.

It was a sea lion, the nearest to me, next to the scuttling waves. It was a human, but the thing was…crisp. Like a piece of Kentucky Fried Chicken, crispy and shedding flakes of skin like a gigantic thick breast. This creature wanted one thing.

–Damn. What can I do?

–Kill. Kill me. Kill me now!

–Oh, hell, I can't do that.

–Look. Look at. Look at me!

The forlorn creature was crawling along without his legs! They were just like legs of a chicken, just bone and black. His hands, or arms, the same, just stomps. His body, just a lunacy, just a torso. He tried to drown himself in the languid ocean, but couldn't stay submerged long enough, coming up for painful air. Even talking was agony.

–Hold. Hold me. Hold me under!

–You sure?

–Hold!

I did what I was told. He struggled, but this would be a relief to him. After, the sea lion lay in the sand, gentle waves washing him. It was over.

But it wasn't over!

The creatures, seeing me act, began to come over to me, about a dozen of them, crying out, begging me to wait for them. I couldn't take it, and ran off the beach, into the car-filled road.

Then, a memory.

Family.

All I could think of was my family: Father, mother, sisters, brothers.

My family in Portland, Oregon. For some reason, I knew the distance from the coast to Portland. I could reach it in only two hours, it was about a hundred miles.

That without shit on the road.

There were trucks, cars, and motorcycles littering the highway. I saw one I liked. It was a 125 Honda. I did have a selection, Suzuki, Yamaha, even a Harley -Davidson, but I passed them all. My first ride was a beat-up 125, and that'd do for me, it brought back some memories. And memories were hard to find, as I mounted the bike, heard the engine rev right up, and took off for...home?

After riding the motorcycle, I got to thinking and maneuvering. I was hungry. For my thirst I had bottled water and I kept them in a loose bag on the 125. I obtained that from cars, pockmarking Highway 26. And 'maneuvering' because there was shit on the road: sea lions long dead, cars, trucks, motor vans, and just junk, as people's last belongings were spread out on the road like a giant had spilled his ultra-size popcorn. I had a full tank of gas, but the hunger was really bad. I had to stop for food. I didn't want to search the cars; the sea lions were really gross. I could only go 40 or 50 miles an hour, the road-shit was so miserable. Then, a little café, and I stopped.

CHAPTER SUB-TWO

APOCALYPSE THERE

I LOOKED AROUND. NOTHING. JUST AN ORANGE CAFÉ.
I opened the screen door. In a rocking chair, was a hideous sea lion. Its feet gone, clothing glued to its atrocious figure, face ebony, and a handgun, in his oversize paw. Beyond the check-out area, a grizzly-bear-sea-lion holding a shotgun in one mauling mitt. His left arm only extended to the bottom of his shoulder. On my left, two more phantasms sat, maybe similarly 'glued' to the chairs, I don't know. I never saw them rise but they both had .22s, one had a scope on the barrel.

I decided to be nonchalant, just like a regular customer.

–Say, how have you fellas been?

One spoke, the rocking chair lion.

–The dead are dead. All living are dying. You look healthy.

–I was just here to get some food.

–There ain't nuthin!

–It seems so. Anything more I can do for you fellas, before I go back out on the road?

–I think you can squirm around on the floor after we shoot you in the legs, we could use some entertainment; it'd be nice to have such fine legs, right boys?

They laughed. And that's all I needed.

As a wink, I had a random fork thrown with incredible speed into the forehead of the lion-o'-rocking. It drove in half-way up the little handle. The sea lion with the shot gun just shot the door off its hinges when he fired, because I was no longer there. I had the gun of the deceased rocking chair ghoul, a .357 magnum and shot the 'gentlemen' with the .22s in both craniums, their unseen brain-viscera I didn't examine (closely). The guy with the shot gun got it in the face, blowing it half-off, then two more in the chest. Two in the chest, one in the head, guaranteed to make 'em dead. I didn't know where that hideous expression came from.

I looked around the place.

Sure enough, no food.

After the killing of my four 'sea-lions' for not-lunch, I felt sick. It was dragon-power that made me so deadly accurate. I had the .357 in the small of my back, not thinking about it at all. I'd never killed any humans before, in this way. Really, like Joan of Arc, I'd never killed anyone directly myself. Joan had to know she sent men to die. By having the dragon-stars here, didn't I do the same? In the battle during the Twins of Triton, didn't I have blood on my hands also?

This was a dream, wasn't it? All a dream?

Yet, I had abilities, and then killed four humans. And that lion on the beach. Is that what having abilities is all about, killing my own? It was atrocious, but I had to defend myself. I had the power of 30 men, maybe more. I began to reassess. Could Lara and Clare and Littorian be, somehow, real?

CHAPTER SUB-THREE
APOCALYPSE EVERYWHERE

I CROSSED THE ROSS ISLAND BRIDGE, EVERYTHING A CARROT-color. Everyone was bringing everything with them when Armageddon happened. I went up the road and arrived at what I thought was my house. I put the kick stand down to the bike. I rambled along on shaky legs to the supposed sidewalk. My home was caved in. I saw four sea lions in the rubble, not moving.

For a long while, I just stared at the immobile nightmares. Then, someone came up to me, standing beside me. I didn't even hear him approach. He was a tall man, dressed in an overcoat, everything black as night.

–Sorry, son. Do they look familiar?

I looked at him. He didn't look like anyone.

–My family?

–Nothing I could do for them, but maybe something I can do for you.

I pulled the .357 on him, placed it against his head. He didn't look surprised at all.

–Sure, you can kill me.

I pull the hammer back.

—But then you'll have to look for more bullets. They can be found; unfortunately, you'll see a whole lotta sea lions before then. That's a very grizzly business, but if you want to, have at it!

I put the hammer down—lightly, and let the pistol fall by my side. I was so defeated; I didn't want to live.

—You, like any writer, are hoping for the honorable way out. You feel powerless, and that's your alienation and estrangement. However, I can help you there.

I put the gun up to my head.

—Good.

I pulled the hammer back, securely back.

—Better. It's over, Brian.

Then, something occurred to me. And I innocently asked the Tall Man.

—Say, how did you know my name was Brian?

The Tall Man did a double take, then hissed in a way that was very, very familiar.

—I don't have time for this shit, your fucking dead!

Lightning fast, he placed a nimble finger over mine on the trigger and fired.

At that same-self instant, squarely in the nick-o'-time, just as the hammer clicked toward the primer of the .357 magnum, my female Black Sword lodged her blade into the little space. The hammer hit her unknown (and unknowable) metal, pinging slightly.

The sea lions disappeared.

The house disappeared, too.

Speak softly of him, and only in The…

And two angry dragons-stars dragged me back to reality, following the lead of my sword, talons seizing both my shoulders.

The Tall Man said "No!" and he became Soreidian, his claw abruptly removed from my forehead.

It was a dream within a dream. One ended.

And almost at once, my .357 magnum skidded away, knocked harmlessly back by my female Black World sword. Terrifically-and-tragically, Soreidian tried to kill me. Larascena picked up the magnum and crushed it into the finest dust. Then, Larascena looked with wide eyes at the knocked-over, Honda 125 motorcycle in the sand. She dismissed this with a dragon harrumph. With her two foremost friends, she muscled her way to work. Maybe the disintegrated gun and motorcycle were real, but it didn't concern me then. My guns fired just when they could, the trigger-happy knives responding to my sudden appearance, knocking Soreidian down.

Littorian, Clareina and Larascena all jumped on Soreidian. More saurians would have beat him up, but there wasn't room. It would have been a blood bath, if I wasn't there to stop it, and that within a few minutes. Littorian actually aimed a massive punch at Soreidian's big masseter muscle. The Lizardanian managed to block the punch with his claws outstretched, but the Warlord was there to bring it home. Larascena seized Littorian's fist and slammed it into Soreidian's sculpted jawline and scored a huge hit, louder than any thunderclap. The Lord of the Lizardanian's fist put Soreidian smack on the beach, making a giant crater. Then Clareina jumped on his chest, squeezing her quadriceps together. Soreidian was going to explode like a tomato can in a saurian vice, damn she was so furious. She then punched her iron fists strongly, stalwartly into his very face with increasing rapidity. His head would have been turned to pulp, but I intervened.

No, no, please, don't hurt him! I'm okay, stop it Clare, please!

I leapt down, and my reptilian wife didn't want to damage me with her city-smashing punches. She stopped because my body was now in the way of her shattering violence. Clare was suddenly motionless and hissed at my act. Soreidian took advantage, leaping out of the sandy indentation. He was about to take off, his wings magically extended, but Littorian was there to wrestle the dragon-star down to the ground again. Littorian, I noted, didn't deploy his wings, he had no need for this. Then he walloped like a god on the chest, throat and face of Soreidian. I intervened with him too, then Soreidian flew off with Danillia and the two sullen companions.

That brought me back to the words of Soreidian, pre-judgement-day-dream. He said they don't 'involve' the families, like on the Sopranos, or some-such. And yet, those 'burned-sea-lions' on my very doorstep, wasn't that an example of my family-used (or used-up)? This gave me the feeling of no hope, that God-approved-indictment of my family. It was only Soreidian's magical incandescence, his phantasm in my ignorant mind. Point is, he did mean to blatantly kill me. I thought that was a bad move. I couldn't believe it, the rage of my saurians I didn't think he'd risk their wrath, setting aside the Black World weapons and my Kerok-inspired pistols? In his defense, Soreidian knew I was trying to get the Crocodilians to take the place of the Lizardanians and the Alligatorians. Of-too-course, I was guilty as charged. I could and would do that, getting one set of protectors over those fleeing it. I thought it was a brilliant plan.

Soreidian thought otherwise.

He was dead set on turning my meaningful-strategy into a teenager-tragedy.

CHAPTER THREE

THE GREAT DRAGON-STAR ROAST

AFTER AGREEING WITH JASON AND RACHEL ABOUT SOREIDIAN's return to the fold of saurians, I approached him on Lizardania. To my surprise, he was a little bit remorseful over the incident. I went to Lizardania on an emergency 'magic' ride from Tiperia herself[5], just to make sure the dreaded 'time' remained almost the same as when I left Earth. Time here, would be (just about) time there! She was always amazing beyond words.

–Would you like me to go with you?

–If you could give Jason, Rachel, Danillia and Soreidian a ride back with you, that'd be all I could ask.

–Take you all together? That's best when handling my juggernaut, 'time' and 'distance.'

---

[5] Just a word about Tiperia. She was Littorian's equal and they were lovers. I first saw the Starfinder as a huge spaceship, at least a mile-long, then as a lawyer, defending Littorian and I at the start of Book III. Then Tiperia shapeshifted into a dragon, and I witness the two of them on Lizardania making the most of each other. Wow, 'nuff said. I didn't know what she was, but she was Littorian's equal. Seeing them in 'intimate motion' I knew why Littorian was so calm all the time. Damn, I would be!

–So, what is your advice, Tiperia?

She had shape-shifted to human form and thought. She had red hair, green eyes, and was very tall. Obviously and completely, she looked magazine-cover-good.

–He's a saurian, your one advantage. He hates you, nothing I can do about that, but he has joined minds with you, Brian. Remind him of the Carcosa time, right here on Lizardania, really right next-door. He's in the gym, so be extremely unctuous. I understand, that he is fully recovered.

This shocked me.

–My lady, this just happened, uh, today! I know you can bend Time and Distance around your index finger, thank goodness for that, but Soreidian had the beatings of three of the most prominent saurians and—

–I don't think Clare is a 'prominent saurian,' Brian.

–She is to me, my lady.

Tiperia just dismissed me, but good naturedly.

–Oh, come now: Soreidian shouldn't be underestimated. He doesn't have any injuries on him, I know. Soreidian and Littorian have never fought.

–Until now, my lady.

Tiperia leaned in, using her elongated fingers, summoning me close, her green eyes flashing.

–You and me: We must prevent it, you have to do something about it, as only you can!

–We must, my—

–We must prevent those two from fighting—because they will kill each other. Talk to him. Get results.

She left me. I had to make this work: I had Jason and Rachel's indorsement. Maybe that was all I needed.

When I came in, the doors were glass, but I had to use all my dragon-force to get them open. They were eight-inch doors, but I never had to push so hard in my life. I tried not to show it.

The six black holes on the straining, hopelessly bending barbells, astonished me the most. They were trapped by a spell of draconian designs. The 'holes' sat (or rather floated) next to Soreidian who was benching them. He had three black 'circles' on each side of the titanic bar he was holding. I saw three other patrons too, two Alligatorians and a Lizardanian. When I walked in, they let their weights fall and all rose. The other reptilians left, without a thought or a word to me, and the door closed. When it did, it locked tightly and there was nothing I could do to open it again. It was Soreidian locking it magically.

–All that is keeping you alive is that I owe you my life. That's not much to go on, if you're wearing the human design.

–My lord: Tiperia, Jason, Rachel, and Danillia have all agreed that this is the best way for you not to fight the other saurians. May I explain the deal to you, my lord?

The incredible weight that Soreidian was pulsing was amazing. All of his strength was being applied, and I was seeing him at 110%.

–Is that so, well, explain away.

–My good lord, well, uh, goodness, how much weight is on each of those, my liege?

–About 3 septillion pounds, human. They are made from collapsed stars. They are safe enough with the kinds of spells I have around them, not to worry.

I gulped.

–So, you are lifting up more than my planet weighs, my sovereign?

I was definitely minding my manners now, key to dealing with any reptilians.

–Right now, I'm lifting 18 septillion pounds, and that with ease, mind.

–Earth weighs in the neighborhood of 13 septillion pounds, my great king.

–I guess I'm lifting more than your neighborhood; so this agreement is?

The saurian increased his raising and falling now, probably just to impress me.[6] I figured if he wanted me impressed, he wouldn't kill me, at least, not right now.

---

[6] I figured right here would be a good place to write more about his philosophy (and his arms!), from <u>Brian Miller: The Theory of Saurian Anarchy</u>, Book Five.

–This is anarchy!

At that, Soreidian stiffened his right arm, making a massive and staggeringly Herculean bulging bicep. It was mountainous and as big as my chest times two, really much larger, 55 or 60 strengthened inches, and almost that around. He 'put' the incredible structure at my up-turned face. I was shocked at the five feet of mega-ultra-muscle before me, a thundering pulsing power that, if pounded down, could earthquake whole <u>nations</u>. It was a massive, green-marble, veined ultra-mega-boulder at full-growth on his masterful arm.

–This is anarchy, this kind of mightiness, and I'm not using magic right now. This is in excess of what Littorian can 'produce.' I can control all matter, for instance, on this or any planet. The permanently alienated human I reject, I have the Tree of Life in this arm—I could destroy you and everything—or create your life forever-more! Anarchy is the stuff of Gods, mind you that! Of course, you will live forever, you have the dragon-elan in your soul, you have consumed the cream of paradise, you have dragon-star blood now. The only impediment left is you can die by violence. I also have another secret for your so-dumb-self: You will become a dragon, a saurian, too. Oh, sure, it will take time. That will be your fate, and I will have nothing to do with all of this. I'd leave you on Earth to die in, really, an instant, and that would be the end of you. Other saurians see it differently, and that's anarchy—I respect the difference, you see? I don't need any 'divine reward' I'll make my own. No one and no-thing can stop me. What do you think of this flex?

–That's the most amazing muscle I've ever seen, and it is gorgeous, my esteemed lord. I've never seen anything so etched and I'm wide mouthed in awe; the peak I'd have to stand on tip-toe to reach, my gracious lord.

–Well trained, well trained. That genuine worship is a real nut-blast. Yes, you do know how to talk to us, your training on this is complete. Let me tell you something about human management and you'll see the connection to anarchy later. The "great" manager is the one who is not encumbered by the outside, one who is brutal to the core, uses people for what they are worth and then throws them away, one who takes the best and leaves the rest (so

—If you would come back to Earth, with your party and endure a roast, then we can all leave, and me to, Katrina, Joan, the 30, all the Alligatorians and the Lizardanians. My lord, to date, I have never seen a saurian lift so much weight. Kukulkan and Teresian have a lot to live up to, given your incredible strength my great lord. Your 20 'enforcement' Lizardanians are not required now, you've won the day, my liege. It will be just words, just a little roast.

The 18 septillion pounds hit the ground, and if it wasn't for the spell, it would have gone through the floor, and, what, through the whole of Lizardania? Who knows?

—My lord, if you'd look at my mental communication with you on Carcosa we—

—Enough. I agree. Don't go on, please!

The bolted glass door unlocked, opened wide. Soreidian rose. Just 'words,' how disagreeable could that be? Instantly, I made secret plans not to be there. My Black World weapons would deliver the juicy goods.

But oh, when you do, what will happen to you, thank God I won't be there to see!

Initially, this 'saurian-roast' wouldn't appease Lara or Clare. Only at my continuous urging did they demure. And I offered them any sexual position they'd like to explore, turning them in my direction that way. I ensured them that Tiperia, Rachel and Jason supported a roast and that Soreidian did agree.

So, after my profound unctuousness, they did think that a good, heart-felt roasting would satisfy. Littorian, though, was good-natured (as well as he could be; he was really pissed off that Soreidian almost offed-me) with talking rather than fatal action. This was one of the reasons I was so comfortable being Littorian's companion. The Lord of the Lizardanians was so comforting and so insightful,

---

ignored and so alone). I hope you have learned at least that, from being with me, I am the opposite of Littorian.

He dropped the flex, but not his comment.

anyone could have been his companion, really. He was like a mother and a father and a best(ess)-friend together as one!

At our base that very night, in the Everglades in Florida, we had our 'Great Dragon Roast,' and what a Roast it was. Soreidian was on a stage, in a giant chair. He didn't 'sit' like a Sphinx, but that wasn't all he was subjected to. Strangely enough, I wasn't there. Soreidian wished, later, that he could have fought the whole bunch of dragons and Black World weapons, he got burned so bad. I'll give you just a part of it, here, but it was really, really bad! Teresian, the Wysterian, went first.

–We have Soreidian here, hello, hello, you dummy worm-and-a-quarter, I knew I kicked something over when I walked in, a shit-kicking-serpent! Ah, Soreidian! Let's just say a few words about you: I just can't believe you are the vice president to Littorian. At least, that's what the humans would call it. You're so disordered, unsound, wandering, walnut-brained, crazy as a loon, a real bedlamite! You retard, you simp, you silly Neely, you little stinking burp, you spouge face, you Jimmy-and-Nelson! I would have torn you all up with one hand, but, alas, there were three other saurians on top of you! You're so lucky I didn't get to your snout. If Brian Miller hadn't intervened, I'd be standing over your grave, throwing flowers down instead of punching your face in. And where the hell is Brian Miller, shitty if he missed this pile-on. Oh, these humans! Is this a roast or what? Fortunately, we have a better fate for them. Soreidian you are a paranoid, shit-dreamer, two-faced, geez, aren't roasts great, not that I couldn't beat the shit out of you anytime), you stupid nut, I've seen younger faces on currency, you odd-imbecile, you big grift, hebetude sucking giraffe dick, piece of shit, your abdominals are totally facile, your arms are weak as an ancient human going to the grave, and your legs are sticks (broken sticks, too). Oh Soreidian, you useless, second fiddle, greasy, huge golem-ghoul, kindergarten-bus-fire-victim, oh, it's so great that the humans have gotten us to be verbal instead of our old sparring matches. Recently Soreidian tried to do some magic. Wow. Watching Soreidian try to do magic is like watching a human retard fuck. I heard he was drunk, and that certain Russians were involved. So, then Soreidian tried to blow into a breathalyzer and the administer said, no, here's the veiny monster cock right over there! The dumb shitass worm passed on the ultra dick and tried to take on the loins of Godzilla! He dislocated his throat and was a veritable shish kabob for the main cross beam of a mega-house, The King's ultra-elephant schlong made him look like a cornhole, rotating shitass! When Soreidian speaks, I have to get out my Ebonics Dictionary, he's a nut-bar gone wild! Then, you know what happened, Godzilla turned him around like a gyrating pinwheel. Look at Soreidian looking a sweet-as-never! Just take it all in, you fat-thing-and-a-half; you feted, festering, charnel house-motherfucker. He's got bowling pins for teeth. Your just such a jerk, please, let Katrina, just one of our little humans here, have a chance.

Katrina mounted the stage and that's not all she mounted.

–Ah, Soreidian, wanna-be Lord of the Lizardanians. How many books will it be before you get there? What's this Book Seven? Eight? Damn, you'll never get there, to be the big boss. I mean look at all the flattened hookers! But I'm not going to get into something juvenile now, calling Soreidian names. Please, we will just leave that to saurians, I mean, the reptilians know you a little bit better than little me. So I'm definitely not going to say he's a stupid, fucking, ignorant, shitfaced, hyper-fat, menacing, threatening, unfriendly, hostile, antagonistic, wicked, nasty, hatefilled, bitter, acrimonious, malign, harmful, injurious, dangerous, noxious, virulent, pernicious, venomous, poisonous, vitriolic, vindictive, chockablock dumbass. I'm trying to let you know, these are just saurians talking, going on and on about your sticky self, wow, they are so cruel, and all the reptilians I've talked to say you're a worthless, grocery bag, fucking dork, but I always defend you saying the camera adds 60 pounds at least and that every saurian has abdominals somewhere lurking around in that stomach fat. Surely (and I do mean to call you Shirley) at least you don't have syphilis, AIDS or gonorrhea, those are all human diseases! You in-breaded hillbilly, gravy-sweating stupid cousin-screwing dumb-ass! His loins should be in the Special Olympics, and, again, those seven-inch teeth would look better on a dumpy horse, a mouth of hacked-off two-by-fours. Most of those teeth are chipped and he looks like a crystal methamphetamine user tripping on crack-cocaine. But yeah, that's my time of dumping on this cum-dumpster, let Clareina have her chance, it's time to get roasted!

Clareina walked to the podium, to the ultra-laughter of many saurians, now that the wine was flowing (and that, dinosaur-large!), and flowing in a good way. She didn't have a sheet of paper, different from the others, and Soreidian shifted uneasily. Maybe some of them were 'forced,' to read, but, on and on, Soreidian didn't think so. He wished he didn't have to be so insulted over-and-over again. Soreidian would have taken Death, just not to be here. Danillia just cringed repeatedly. Rachel and Jason, bagel mouthed. Their own Black World weapons were similarly 'displaced.'

–Soreidian, so glad you decided not to fight me but to be verbally insulted. I guess Brian polished your ass for that! I'm glad you weren't sliding your minuscule dick up some human's back parts. But sometimes seriously folks, Soreidian's loins look like the fairer sex, *writ large*. You vodka-drunk, worm-and-a-half, how I'd love you under my shiny, seven-inch claws! If you had to go human, seek out someone who can see their cock when they are peeing. You look like a toad scratching his own microscopic wee-wee. No offense for companions and saurians other than shit-kicking Soreidian. You are a big, ghoulish, morbid, horrifying, macabre, morose, saturnine, boring sub-slime-worm. And that's just your good side! They say you have a morbid muscle or two? Look at you! Just foundering around like a spastic, massive ape on a stage. And look, Brian Miller: You are looking to get Soreidian here for insults? Wow, you're the man. Sad, too. You should be a dragon-star, I'm just waiting on the day. Where is Brian Miller, that's all I want to know. Back to you Soreidian, hopeless snake-without-clothes, you gay weeble. But let's turn our corn-cobbled Soreidian-ass over to Larascena!

Larascena smacked hands with Clare, looking to get it on.

–Yes, Soreidian is still here my happy, shiny people, just look at him. I'm struggling to think about what's been said about him, looking for what isn't true. Sorry, it all is! I hear you watch porn almost all the time we don't see you in dialogue. And that's quite a lot, I can tell you that! I wonder if you watch humans or aliens? Humans it would be, if you want to see your own junk looking normal, simian sized, right? You are such a shitty saurian, I'm embarrassed to speak to you, you have bolts in your skinny neck. You twisty drooling drunken dork, your dream is to titty screw a Crocodile. Not a Crocodilian, you have to move up the evolutionary ladder. And it's good to see that Soreidian wormed-up in here, that's good for a shifty snake! You planet-ruining-dick-sucker, you heartless fucking-piss-tank. Let me turn you back over for a ram-rod from the real Lord of the Lizardanians, prepare your pucker hole for another king size anaconda!

Littorian seized the podium in a draconian way.

–I've never had a deputy slipping on his own non-existent shoelaces like Soreidian. He tried to end my companion's life, but I can forgive him. I'd like to kill him, but my companion says no. I understand that Brian Miller kicked your silly ass when we rescued Joan of Arc, right? Oh, I would have loved to be there. Here's what I'm going to do, another footnote, illustrating that you got the jack-ass-shit beat out of you by Brian Miller[7]. And where is my companion, now? Yep, that's done. Oh, Soreidian, what did

---

[7] Just before I left Rouen, when the sun was almost down, as I left town to go to the castle, I got five-flagged in my unsuspecting face. It'd been a long time since someone punched me. But it was a human's sock, it didn't 'knock my block off,' like a saurian's talon-filled strike would do.

Oh, no.

I didn't even fall or stagger back. It was full in the face, but no blood issued forth from my lips. I had the blood of three leading dragons in me

I call you before? My *da fuq*, fruit loop, space cadet, yes, that was

---

now, and that wasn't affected by my travel-in-time, and <u>someone</u> was going to get-it-<u>bigly</u>!

–Now we can have that fight, Brian. I'm going to make you suffer, but good. I just wish Danillia was here, she'd like this very much.

It was the shape shifted Soreidian. He'd changed into a priest, no less! He was bald as a harsh purge, too.

–Just my chance to lash out at the Catholic Church, thank you Soreidian, you cheeky shill!

The faux priest smiled.

–Correlation doesn't equal causation, Brian.

–In this case, it does, and I'm going to kick your Catholic correlation butt!

–And you, un-cultured sodomite, come on!

–You shape-shifted piece of shit, stepping on my every-punchline, you'd betta recognized my gangsta, Soreidian!

The shapeshifter thought he was <u>still</u> a dragon-star, almost invincible. As Soreidian he certainly was. Now, not so much at all. I sent all my Black weapons away, with a wink to them. And so did Soreidian! The worst move he's ever made. He had no mental ability to call his Black Sword and other weapons back! His Black Sword knew this, but the shape-shifted dragon didn't.

Weapons dismissed (my own Black World sword with a snicker and wink), the priest hit me three times in the stomach, three in the face, full force. My abs were very strong, and still no blood peppered my face.

–That'd be it? This is for Joan of Arc!

I hit the shape-shifted priest and he landed 10 feet away. I wasn't done with him yet.

Half unconscious at my first blow, I straddled his chest and hit him continuously in the face. I could have punched him through the ground completely, making a grave for him right there, but I held back. Splattering his mug, I made stirred-up strawberry pie out of his vulnerable jaw.

When his cheek bone did appear, caked in milky-blood, I stopped. My dragon veins said to finish him, my humanity held me at bay. If he died here in the past, he'd never live as a dragon again. I knew that, but 'absolute violence' was not in me; some violence, that, but not enough to finish anyone.

I got up.

Soreidian didn't.

it. You've gone way too far, but, of course, my companion has preserved your life. But, dear me! We have 'roasts' coming from so many others, gang way, come on, companions and saurians, he's all yours!!!

He was barely conscious. He tried to rise but couldn't, his black robes red, too.

–Come on don't get up for me. I've got the most powerful saurian blood in my bones—and Littorian's too. An ode to Lara. I hope you've learned something about being hurt like all-buggery, Soreidian. You're a little French human here-and-now, so get used to it. Shape-shifted, you've got no dragon in you at all! I'll send you back some help, damn, you need it. You just got pwned!

CHAPTER FOUR

STAR'S FREEZING, BURNING THROUGH ME

THE COTTON-WOOL EXISTENCE OF DRAGON-STAR-LOVE, SAURIAN wings, locking me down in ruthless and passionate embrace, I couldn't possibly give that up. Even now I'm perplexed as to how I'd 'forgotten' about my affairs with my reptilian wives through Soreidian's hideous dream.

It's no wonder that my Trinity would have been the death of that Lizardanian, Soreidian, were I not there. I didn't realize how much I loved my wives, and the price of giving them up was too much. I'd die for them; life isn't worth going on without them by my side.

CHAPTER FIVE

JOAN OF ARC GONE WILD—
& RIGHTLYWRONG

ALL THIS TIME, JOAN OF ARC WAS TRYING TO ARRANGE (IN A ZANY way) time travel to save the Donner Party. She didn't want to put pressure on Anakimian, her Alligatorian companion.

For me, I was reading <u>The Indifferent Stars Above</u>, by Daniel James Brown, just trying to get an insight on what fascinated Joan of Arc about the Donner Party. They started with 80, and then there was 40, gruesome cannibalism was the history written. I cringed on page 193, Chapter 11, "Madness," and could really go no further. It reminded me of Lincoln Beach in Oregon. Though things were 'just barely better' between Soreidian and me, my relations with Danillia were much the same. The 'ouch' from the Roast, Soreidian hated. Danillia wanted to kill me, just like she said to me back in high school, at our first meeting:

"It wouldn't do to have you harmed…before your time!"

I guess Danillia would be competing with Death Incarnate and anybody related to the pirates of Book III, in gunning for me.

Right after my reading, I conferred with the Maid. Jehanette assured me, and I saw it true, that she loved her companion. Anakimian saved her from the flames. He bore her to future-Earth, and was trying to make her 'settle in.' They'd even taken a trip to France, and Joan looked in amazement at what the Catholic church 'thought' of her now. Before condemned and going straight to Hell; now, a Saint! Maybe thesis, antithesis and synthesis should be looked at again.

Joan cried out to me at one time:

–Did you know that 50% of the people on the Donner Party were under 18? It's a high crime to leave them where they are, they had no time to experience real life. Can you help me Brian?

–Geez, Jehanette, can't we take our time? They have passed on and the time it takes to get the time travel organized won't make any difference to those kids! Really, if we think about it, can't we 'go back in time' to save the original 30 companions and then not go get Joan of Arc, you yourself, to organized them?

–Saints perceive us, that doesn't make a lick of sense to me.

–Of course not. I really don't explain my positions very well. I will try to encourage the dragon-stars to see your point of view. Just give me a little time, Joan!

CHAPTER SIX

END OF SAURIAN INTERVENTION

ENDING SAURIAN INTERVENTION BY RETURNING 'THE OUTPOST' TO human control didn't concern me much. It was nearly done, Littorian just had to hand over the keys (and there were no keys).

Soreidian was right, after all. I thought about this with everything in a "dimensional state" on my desk, as recommended by my female Black Sword. Too much math for me. It didn't look like much: All my papers and books, and just 'incidentals' all in three piles. The incidentals included my desks, chairs, bookcases, file cabinets, and other truck-n-junk.

I did intend for the Crocodilians to guide humanity on a non-violent course through my Asian-companion intervention. I knew what kinds of benign-interference with natural-nature a companion could and would give. The companions were gentle but a little squirrely. We were compassionate yet rebellious. We have clever, eye-candy-teenagers, but they were a bit clumsy. Still, better than adults!

CHAPTER SEVEN

BETERIENNA GONE LAZARUS

LARASCENA 'GATHERED' HERSELF, ALL HER HIDDEN ABILITIES, AND that is saying something! All her gorgeous, invigorating strength was going to be applied to the healing process. Clare, now studied-up on the ancient Alligatorian body (and soul) was generating all that a Lizardanian dared possess, in a "curing power" knowing no bounds.

Tiperia granted passage as a Starfinder to Alligatoria and to the Planet at the End of the Universe, for another 'rescue.' No time could pass on any of the worlds, a 'second' here would be a 'second' there. Earth, Lizardania, Alligatoria or Crocodilia were all subject to the Queen of Time. Space, (dreaded) Time and Distance were Tiperia's Trinity, and, like a ring on Lord of the Rings, indeed, The One Ring, she bent it to her will. That analogy is flawed, of course, that ring was meant for Evil, but here, it was meant to save Beterienna from the Abyss of No Return and get Sheeta and Terminus off that far-away planet and back with us. Not only this, but the addition of Littorian, the Lord of the Lizardanians, was just a little icing on the cake and I knew we wouldn't fail.

Lara had just this to say, just a little ramble.

–Your King of this land is just a pawn, and he's judged, really, by his councilors. And I know what a pawn can become—in chess—if it makes it down to the far end of the board. This is outlandish for an anarchist, the sooner all saurians are released from Earth, the better. This hierarchy stuff will one day get you all killed. The lingering suffering of a Limited Nuclear War (if you're lucky) has to make all humans cringe. Limited isn't limited you know, it's really limitless! And this is precisely why now is the time to awaken Beterienna! We are talking about the near-dead and the post-dead. I have to make something alive and she is it, an ancient Alligatorian!

–Your wisdom is amazing and dazzling to me, my queen.

–As it should be.

Tiperia and Littorian had a great time watching Beterienna beating the hell out of Clare and Lara in her panoply of 'living again,' just going crazy on the two of them. The two reptilians thought they could handle the post-life flowing from Beterienna and waived everyone back. The Lizardanian was assured that she'd have an advantage on Beterienna, an Alligatorian. A Lizardanian could produce enough strength to manage such a beast, so Clare was comforted. Not true here. The only thing preventing her from almost killing the two healers was the sudden appearance of her professor husband, Beterian. I had summoned him secretly when we first got to Alligatoria, to come to the Mortuary Center immediately. Memory came back, just when she had Lara under her mighty foot, and Clare raised helplessly up in her ignorantly, non-avenging claws, covered with new, rich saurian blood. Littorian spoke, now that Beterian showed up to spoil the party.

–Glad we weren't called in to help, right everyone?

But it was Right Two Hands that spoke in a spirited way.

–I could have at least landed Beterienna in her own crater using all my three rounds, but, like you say, the call to help never came.

Lara and Clare were left to recover themselves, while Beterienna hugged Beterian, each talking frantically.

–Beterienna, I welcome you back into the breathing domain. I am (the recovering) Warlord of Alligatoria, Larascena, and this is Clareina, the Lizardanian. We are Lara and Clare to you, my dear. It is good to get you back from the Water World. Explanations can wait, but I will think everything to you, anon. Would you like to come with Tiperia to begin (and draconianly) complete our saving of Sheeta and Terminus? They escaped through Time rescuing Joan of Arc, out on a far world. Brian, what are you doing all-the-day, give them a book to read on that, Brian Miller: Joan of Arc and the Dragon-Stars, you guys study up!

Beterienna recovered herself fully.

–Yes of course I will help you. Oh, thanks for the book, Brian, we will read that on our way, is that okay Beterian? Clare and Lara, you have saved my life from the Abyss. Anything and everything are of course yours, if it is within my power to make it happen. Again, sorry for injuring you, I was definitely not myself. I see now that your teenager was the only adult in the room, with his summoning of my husband, and I'm so sorry for knocking you all around. I was not who I am currently. I'm sorry for this, I just didn't recognize.

Larascena was quick to the point.

–I rather liked it, it's good to taste my own blood, bravo to you, Beterienna.

–It's Beteri, to you, Lara.

I spoke, then.

–And to me?

–All three of you; maybe you are the Trinity to me!

Jagged rocks around us, just as we prepared to depart from Alligatoria to find Sheeta and Terminus, Larascena saw it first. Drogon was flying over, and he cradled Daenerys Targaryen.

–Well, Jon Snow be damned, broken wheels be smashed, and iron swords melted, look who's here!

Bewildered, I inquired to Larascena.

–My esteemed Lara, what's going on?

—Game of Thrones, don't you know? See that dagger in Daenerys? Maybe it's not too late, will you help me Clare?

Drogon landed, wind whirled around us, and he released Daenerys from his talon, looking hopefully on. Clareina grabbed the blade in Daenerys and crushed it to dust. Together, both the Lizardanian and the Alligatorian examined and touched the incision area (which was extensive for a knife injury).

I wasn't sure what Clare and Lara could do, they were both exhausted from the effort to get Beterienna cured, but, wink-quick, the girl came around! Drogon let out a loud cry of joy as Daenerys rose. Lara had a quick assessment.

—Well, soonest begun, soonest done!

Talk about a fifth wheel, boy, I was! I smiled and immediately when over to Ms. Targaryen and bowed to her.

—My lady, since I'm a human too, I'm hoping to give you some support. Can I introduce you to Larascena, the Warlord of all Alligatoria and Clareina, a young Lizardanian? Obviously, they've used combined power to save you! I'm Brian Miller, a companion (among other things but I'll give you a chance to talk).

—Last thing I can remember is Jon Snow. He stabbed me? Because he thought I'd be the daughter of the Mad King, and, what was he thinking that I'd kill everyone?

—My queen: I'm perplexed. I'm afraid I didn't watch Game of Thrones. I guess we are all at the sideways dumpster fire of mercy of some stupid writer, somewhere/how? Getting back to Jon Snow, uh—

—I really don't wish Drogon had fired him.

—He didn't, my lady, as I understand.

—That's good—because I want to kill him myself.

—Then you'll just be confirming yourself as a mini-Mad King, my queen?

—And with a little, cute-something on it, please? I'm not going to kill anyone who doesn't need it. Drogon, we have some work to do?

Interestingly, during our little aside, Drogon wasn't in attendance. He was confirming with Larascena.

—I think you did the right thing, bringing your queen here, very good. I know about your designs too, very appropriate, I think you will please her well. I'm married to Clare and Brian Miller. We have a really good time! I think you'll owe me twice, because I've something for Daenerys that she won't soon forget.

At that, she whisked over one of Clare's knives. This particular knife lost his own Paper, Scissors, Rock contest. So, he had to go with Daenerys. I just hoped the knife would do the right thing. We'll see.

CHAPTER EIGHT

SHEETA AND TERMINUS
(LAZARUS 2.0)

—SHEETA AND TERMINUS MUST BE FOUND AND DEFINITELY SAVED, and I don't want to hear anything about it! It must be done now. We have Beterienna coming along for this adventure. And Littorian too. And I know just where they are. At least five to rescue Sheeta and Terminus? Shit, they are rescued already. I'm thinking a duo is in order.

Berteri, willing to make up for her crimes of beating the crap out of Lara and Clare, really wanted to help.

Tiperia got everyone there, right away. On the far-world, aliens were sieging a huge mountain, I was interested in diplomacy, communicating with the aliens. This effort was supervened by Littorian himself.

—I'm monitoring your thoughts, and what is this? Wow, this is something new, from the minds of the aliens? A bot? A virus?

—My lord, this is entirely new to me?

—Your own dragon-star blood should keep you from the ill effect of these little killer-thoughts, these mental germs, don't worry. But

I think the Warlord and Beteri have something more sinister in mind, right?

The two Alligatorians, now functioned as a team.

–Everyone of you, stay on Tiperia. We will do the rescue ourselves, okay? These silly aliens besieging our comrades won't do with diplomacy? Very well, and then-some. We have something more 'dragonkin' in mind anyway.

I didn't know what was coming, but if you have ever, in your travels, seen the Animatrix and the machines warring against mankind, then you are lucky because that's just what these two dragons faced. The alien machines and ships were taken right out of the illustrator's drawings for "The Second Renaissance: Part II" on the Animatrix, an addition to the Matrix series. It's at youtube. com, and I have the utmost respect for the Wachowski's work and the directors around them. And I've got to give credit where it is due! The pyramids, though, were upside down, firing green light rays at the mountain. It made sense to me why a dragon-star would use a mountain as his final redoubt. Terminus had a shield around the mountain, and that shield was weakening. Terminus was held up there, taking all that fire, while Sheeta was the foot-soldier, running around killing all the aliens she could find. The dragons used their Black World swords to protect these two worn-out friends, and then the angry saurians got to work. It was over in less than a minute.

I had a great view as I had my own female Black Sword go over the planet, with Tiperia's behest, to see it all. I used my binoculars from the Water World, and I got to witness everything. It was a super-Apocalypse, and there was nothing left of this world, it was dragon-fire dead. Lara used a flame that had no equal, and it was deep red. Berteri had a white flame that was designed to kill all the brains of the aliens, and thorough she was, too. I think the flames were produced by magic. All the same, nothing lived after. I was flabbergasted at the destruction. Terminus was using a shield over the mountain, and that was the only thing still in place, it was a very light green structure. Sheeta stopped with her little war, nothing left to slay. Terminus was overjoyed.

All went back to Tiperia, and a celebration commenced. I didn't feel shitty about these stupid aliens. Who would?

CHAPTER NINE

HORROR AT 32,008 FEET & RODS FROM GOD

KEROK NEEDED TO SETTLE HIS RIDER, SAYING THE FOLLOWING, JUST lightly, in dragon-flight.

–Now then: My bright teeth are a modest six-and-a-half inches long and I can expand my jaw to around four feet—six feet if I dislocate myself. I can do that, but in your case, I don't think it's necessary. My other physical features fall a little short of my comrades. My biceps are under 40 inches, my peak is modest, and I really don't care to 'work' on my body any further. I'd rather read a transmission or a book!

Nausicaa solemnly nodded, only partially giggled.

The joint military project was taken on by the Russians and the Americans. It was 'practiced' on Kerok at the Novaya Zemlya Island in the Russian Arctic Sea. As they approached, draconically (of course), the Alligatorian had a moment of stall in the sky!

–I'm sensing some radiation in the air here; I'm going to have to establish an atmosphere around you. You know what height we're at?

The wind then died appreciably as the reptilian established an atmosphere.

–Dangerous, my lord? And what's our height?

–For you, my dear, and we've just begun this companionship. And our distance above the Earth is 32,008 feet, really high.

–And that's *after* drinking your blood, my grace?

And Kerok was silent, then friendly again.

–I've a confession for you now. I'm the weakest of all saurians you will meet, probably ever (I mean, among the adults). And that number totals 13, emphasizing how unlucky you are.

Nausicaa assured him.

–If you want to give me an atmosphere, so be it! And don't be so pagan, my lord!

Nausicaa believed that Kerok's life was worth more than honor, integrity, uprightness, <u>anything</u> dealing with words of any kind. This was a revocation to her, and really a revolution against her own DNA!

Nausicaa considered quietly for a time.

–I had no idea that you where the very weakest of your race, my good lord. Because you are the wisest, however, if offered the choice with the foreknowledge, I would again serve you my king, if you'd have me. With that, my great lord, on the way to a fight I don't want you to have, I will tell you of the 47 Ronin of my country, Japan. First, I'm not really Japanese, but my world had a Japanese culture, just like Earth. I'm from the 'Zombie World,' as Brian likes to call it. But on this planet, I consider Japan to be home, on with the story?

–Oh, fantastic, this is better than I had planned. Human knowledge, you'll find me an empty cup, waiting for your words, my sweet companion.

–As you say, my lord, are you ready for this?

–I'm going to give you level-flight, I'm so excited on this level of knowing. Yup, I'm going to hold a level pattern, I'm so interested in what you have to say. Hold on to my fin firmly, okay?

–I'll hold on to and caress more than that, my lord. This fin is a foot and a half long? Hopefully you've got something more, uh, erect for me to place my hand on?

–You mean both hands, and your two feet too. I've been likened to have a massive hammer just as long as a cross beam to any house, and the girth is as thick as a tree trunk, too. "Jes' sayin'" as Brian Miller, uh, says. Now, go on, go on, and I'm not trying to push and pressure you into anything, so to speak.

–I'm going to get all wet with talk like this. I know your hung like any massive Mastodon, but I've a story to tell. Now, the Ronin, my lord, is translated as 'waves,' waves without a master. In my country, folks are disciplined, and, I am afraid, hierarchical, too. We have different social classes performing different functions. Maybe you'll think we have parasitic classes. You will have to live with this form of DNA in me; but my DNA can be added to or even bent severely. I leave that up to you. I know you will never be 'superior' to anyone or anything. Kerok, I know right now that you are the purest, and this 'second chance' with these silly militaries, I think they can miss it and find something else. Say we won't go?

–Nah, I'll take them all on, don't worry about me. On with the story now, this is about samurai, right?

–Yes, a samurai is "the one who serves." I will now cite 'The Ako Incident,' my lord, I'm trying to be a samurai to you, and I hope you'll let me. I follow Bushido, that is, samurai code. A mere 'picture' of the Ronin only reveals half the story. The power comes from being a minority, and that's where the courage comes from. I'm aware of Larascena's view of "courage," and I think it's not fair to judge humans like dragons.

–Do get on my dear girl!

–At your esteemed command, my gracious lord. This takes place around 1700, and is true, to my mind, my star-mighty-dragon. You don't mind if I hold on to your arm like this, wow, you're all muscle, but you've heard this before. My story is from feudal Japan, and you know about all of that, studying economics, as you do.

The samurai class was struggling to keep its proud individuality and the Western groups just kept interfering with their capitalistic bullshit. My country was at peace for almost 100 years, and stuff was steady and on-course, of course (setting aside the earthquakes and tsunamis). So, Lord Asano Naganori was chosen by the Shogun, Tokugawa Tsunayoshi, to be one of the several daimyo—

–Hold on, my companion, what's a daimyo?

–Uh, my lord: a powerful Japanese feudal lord. The "dai" means "large" and the "myo" stands for private land. Can I go on, my lordship?

–Yes, please.

–Alright: So, they were invited to Edo (today, that's Tokyo), to meet with and, well, companion with, so to speak, the royal family's envoys. Assigned to assist Lord Asano was the Shogun's highest-ranking member of protocol, Kira Yoshinaka. He was going to show the Lord what to do, with proper court etiquette. But they didn't get on well, my lord Kerok. They grew to hate each other, regrettable, but true. Kira wanted to get paid, but Lord Asano thought he was only doing his duty. I guess capitalism reigns even here. Kira wanted to get paid for his instruction. Kira thought it was disrespectful, and he thought he was superior to Asano and—

Kerok interrupted and made Nausicaa close her mouth by bouncing up and down, very abruptly.

–We have a thing here in saurian society called sparring matches, my gentle female.

–I was just getting to that, my impatient, but esteemed lord.

–Do get! You go girl.

–Very well. Kira embarrassed Asano everywhere, all the time. Just before the main ceremony, the two were talking. Kira called Asano a country piece of dung with no manners. That set Asano off and he lunged at Kira with his sword and struck him on the face. This was a great offense, my lord Kerok. After, Lord Asano was questioned. Asano said he should have killed Kira. The Shogun heard the story. He was very merciful and he—

Again, with the awkward harrumph-in-the-air, Kerok's wings dropped, making her mouth snap shut so fast her teeth rattled.

–Merciful, you see there? You see it? Damn, Brian Miller should see now that his Asian racist stuff is caught short with this <u>merciful</u> act. Brian would have concluded the worst about this story, he is so racist about it all. I'll tell him about the mercy shown, hell, I'll just think it to him, now what was it, Nausicaa?

–My air honchoing lord, it was Hara-kiri.

–Huh? What's that?

–My lord, it's like Seppuku.

–What's that?

–Disembowelment, my sovereign.

–Oh, no they didn't—

–They honorably slit their bellies open with a knife, abdomen gashing and slashing, my lord.

–Oh, hell to the no!

–Can I go on, my benign but grossed-out dragon-star?

–Well, if you must, that's a crying shame, though, shit maybe he's right, goddamn DNA; well in time, he'll be wrong again, thank God for time!

–Anyhow, my lord, the Shogun said the Lord Asano could commit Hara-kiri, but added to the sentence, the sum of well, $50,000 (or something like that). When the judgement was announced at Asano's palace, his retainers, now Ronin (without a master) thought about what they should do. They surrendered the palace peacefully, but they were in a planning phase, and some kind of revenge. Kira knew about the loyalty felt and became paranoid. He was on guard all the time and increased his security. Asano's men just went 'balling' at the local brothels, putting on quite a show as to their disinterest on taking revenge. That was 47 men out of 300 warriors, by the way. Two years past, Kira thought he was safe enough. On December 14, 1702, with snow everywhere, cold night in Edo, the Ronin attacked! The Ronin fought and then they found Kira in an outhouse. Kira was given the opportunity to commit Hara-kiri and he—

Once again, Kerok did a snap in the air, bouncing up and violently down, making Nausicaa's lower jaw ring closed. Nausicaa thought she almost bit her tongue off, the shimmy was so sudden.

—Damn, you Japanese are—

—Nipponese, my friend. If you're going to insult us, let's use the proper terms. In fact, 'Nipponese,' is not even right. And if you hiccup us up and down again, my friend, I'll discontinue the story of the 47 Ronin, you'll have to hear the Ako Incident from Sheeta and—

—I'm not going to insult you, my friend. Do you care about this life?

—If it's an honorably led life, yes. In your case, honorable or not, I care about you, Kerok!

—Go on, let's have the last!

—Very well, my lord. Kira's response to the request to commit Seppuku didn't come soon enough for the Ronin, and he was decapitated, and his head placed in a bucket. The sword used to saw off Kira's head was the same one Asano had used two years prior. The Japanese Emperor said they could all commit Seppuku and they are buried on Sengaku-ji, along with their master. This is the best example of courage, honor and loyalty you'll find if you visit our homeland, and I do encourage that before we finally leave. They sacrificed for what they thought was right. I know, with time, we see truths different than now. I know I'm from a different world, but Japan is still Japan, even if it's on Earth, if you see what I mean. But, with our shortened life span, I think that can be forgiven by the gods, by you, my lord dragon-star.

Kerok flew on, level-flight, before he spoke.

—I'll take care not to damage your DNA, but I'm sure you know what is up with us, these days. Wanting to make you dragons, wishing to be off this world, and caring about our companions, those teenagers who can last, well, forever? Still, I don't see what caused the overall 'weakness' in the 47 Ronin story. Can you elaborate on this, please?

–I know your plans, my lord. Whether you can realize them, well, that's kind of up-in-the-air (like we are). And as to 'weakness' maybe the 300 warriors had only 47 that spoke so openly of committing Hara-kiri, and that's where the 'weakness' lies?

Kerok considered, then dismissed it.

–The fact that you end the last sentence with a question mark means you don't know yourself. We should look further at the 'weakness' you and I. Have you seen Claymore? This was animation, 'anime' and it ran for just one season.

–I'll have to look that Manga up, my liege.

–The girl, Clare, in that story was the 47th in The Organization, the 'weakest' Claymore (all the women carry a big, supersize sword), and yet, Clare was the strongest of all, you should look this up. Anyway, I do see a parallel here. Our militaries await! Let's see if they have improved on finishing off a saurian, the suspense is killing me, I hope it'll last!

And the weapons employed where phenomenal. Railguns with 950 millimeter rounds (over 37 inches) swarmbots, plasma force fields and "ray guns,' with lasers galore, a .75 caliber Gatling gun, the largest tank in the world, helicopters and fighter planes, anti-tank rounds, missiles and then the 'Tsar Bomba,' a hydrogen bomb dropped down an iron tube and, finally, a 'Rod from God,' dropped from a satellite into the very mouth of Kerok at supersonic-plus speed! The militaries set the Tsar Bomba aside, thinking the Rod from God would be enough to finish the reptilian. This was a kinetic bombardment. Kerok had to maneuver, maw open, to get underneath the rod, which was amazing.

Just by-the-way, Kerok was the 'main saurian' behind curing Japan of their nuclear mishap with the 2011 tsunami that devastated Fukushima, Fukushima Daiichi. Fukushima means 'lucky island'

and it's very lucky that Nausicaa was companioned to Kerok. 16,000 people plus lost their lives in the tsunami. Kerok looked at the problems having a readymade spell, put all the radiation into a little box he carried with him. Then, he went to all the hospitals, curing cancer and radiation like a god-among-men. He also designed a spell to use on the Pacific Ocean, destroying all man-made radiation. I think, later, he disposed of this killer-of-humanity on one of the space-rides he gave to Nausicaa. I, Brian Miller, did suggest he help, but it was Nausicaa that made it happen. Since my struggle with Soreidian, I've become humbler. So there.

Chernobyl was much, much harder on Kerok, and he had to call in other saurians to address the human sick and the overall environment. The people fixing the nuclear problems were called "the liquidators" and all those associated with them needed treatment. Over 300,000 people needed his help. Kerok made a decision on an Alligatorian over-all spell. Truth was, he didn't want to work that hard. So, every hospice, every hospital, had a dragon-call. Things were better, all radiation gone, but the lessons of the 'lasting dead' die hard. Of the 'long dead,' the dragon-stars could do nothing to bring them back. The soldiers considered Kerok a god and honored him mightily. He didn't like that; it went far beyond the kind of fawning he <u>did</u> like. He was the wisest saurian of all. They weren't God Almighty, and they knew it. The Russians were more than paid back in their defense of Soreidian during the Twins of Triton adventure.

Incidentally, on Kerok's request to go and visit the Chernobyl reactor to obliterate the radiation in the air, the Russian leader, Mr. Putin, had an unusual condition.

Nausicaa had a concerned look, and her Asian eyes went appreciably up. Japan tried to have good relations with Russia, so she decided to meet him halfway.

–If Kerok is willing, be it so, just ask him. I mean right now, we are leaving this minute for the Ukraine. Still willing to go, no guarantees as to your safety?

Putin saw the dragon, seeing it was now or never.

–I will ask him through you, please let's go, I wanted to visit Belarus just next door!

And that's how Putin got a dragon ride, he sat forward of Nausicaa as they took a seat on Kerok's generous, sinuous back. Putin was having a marvelous time, appreciating that all the radiation would be gone soon, impressing the media, as he mounted the dragon star. She nodded to Kerok, granting a forward position to the Russian leader, wanting Putin to see everything.

And just to say thanks for all his work getting rid of the plethora of radiation, the militaries wanted a re-do! Not satisfied with their attempt to kill the Wysterian, the humans regrouped to kill the weakest of the saurians, Kerok! The closer the dragon star got to the Russian base, the more Nausicaa wished to be somewhere else.

–My lord, I'm not saying that you're not wise in accepting this industrial-military-redux on you, but I—

–Don't worry, my child, this is just to show off to you, you see, as the flimsiest of the reptilians, just let me show-boat a little. Now then: There is something that Jamie Johnson's "Born Rich," will never have (ever!). You know what that is, Nausicaa?

–What's that, my Lord?

–To be a companion! That means all humans have to die—the leveler of all things, my human! But you! You are a <u>companion</u>, you've drunk dragon-star blood, meaning you will live forever. What could be better? Mean(<u>mean</u>)while, the 1% have no place here. I know all the saurians, the ones having the new 30 now and all reptilians despise the 'well off.' It's a cry against anarchy, having the means to rule over others. If I only gave a fucking shit about the "philosophy" of the 1% indicated in that Johnson documentary, I'd kill all the rich, as a nod to the penniless. Give all their money away to the homeless? See what the grave 'gives' them, rich bitches. But I don't give a care about the mass of humans, only my companion and a few (lucky) others. You'll have to do the rest. That's Brian Miller's cross to bear.

The Air Force colonel at the base was to have operational command of the procedure. The generals, Russian and American, just stood aside, as a little group. Nausicaa Lee grew more nervous as the introductory brief ended. So far, the weakest saurian had withstood all the military elements thrown against him. This was the last part of the test.

–I understand, for this scenario, that a three-foot-wide, 2,000-pound rod will be shot down from a satellite and I don't need to hear about the kinetic energy or how fast past the speed of sound it can go, and all that blah-blah. I will get under this little rod, with my mouth open. Remember that I'm the weakest saurian that you can test. Tell you what. The Black World Swords won't let the blast wave exceed a mile across, okay? I can take care of any injuries that are made known to me. You can all relax, but I don't think you will.

The Rod was fired and impacted right in the mouth of the saurian! The Black World Sword (Kerok's) prevented the blast wave, as ordered. He didn't like testing the reptilian this way either, but grudgingly demurred.

Binoculars to eyes, the Air Force colonel was ecstatic and very much surprised.

–I see him, I see him, about half a mile away, in that massive crater! Air Force all the way, right gentlemen? Damn, it was level ground before, but now, that's a dead saurian if I've never-ever seen one. That rod from Jeezum' Hood Crow is three quarters into his entire body, it's just about to bulge out of his guts!

Surprising even himself at his off the cuff (and then some) rant, the Air Force colonel added but this:

–He does have the finest set of guts, I mean, pulsing abdominals, that I've seen on a dragon my lady.

–Thank you, that's the finest thing I've ever been told by someone representing the Chair Force, I mean, the Air Farce, I mean—

The Colonel cut in.

–I won't say that the Air Force bombed two targets in Japan with nukes, no I won't say that.

–I think it was the <u>Army</u> Air Force, right?

–Technicalities, my dear.

Binocular-less, Nausicaa grew worried, blew the colonel off, and thought desperately to Kerok, sensing nothing back. With the plethora of dragon-star blood flowing richly in her veins, she could see details like an eagle.

In a panic now, she was about to reach out to all saurians and me, Brian Miller, and everything and everyone in her newly designed telepathy, when Kerok came into her mind.

Oh, don't wet yourself, my silly girl! I'm okay, I'm just trying to get these military types to see my post-performance, then we will majestically, dragonly-go. Geez, your spoiling it all with your mental teetering! Just don't say anything, just wait—you don't see me breathing or winking or anything, right? My belly should look quite bloated and pale as a dead fish, oh, my companion, I'm just playing possum!

Seeing the weakest Alligatorian with her wide, green eyes, now enhanced by his own dragon-star blood, she stopped her telepathy. She then smiled widely. The colonel noticed this. Then the Japanese girl affected a stony look, as the Air Force overseer thought she rightly should.

–Sorry, young lady, but you'll have to go looking for another companion. Seems like our power defeated at least the weakest saurian. In retrospect, I'm responsible for that saurian's death. Again, sorry but I guess he had it coming.

–You knew he was the weakest one?

– Sure thing, I knew he was weakest, and so what? We've got to report some kind of progress to the President and the world there, girl.

–Girl? Uh-huh. It's not really grief it's a little gloating, too, right? You are proud to put a well-meaning reptilian down.

–If the shoe fits, wear it and be smug. It's Biblical. The serpent got put down in the Bible, you know, literally underfoot.

Nausicaa had enough.

–No. Lemme out there, get out of the way, Air-shit-birds!

Immediately, the colonel gave word to restrain the companion. Her hand went up immediately towards the Black World weapons. They didn't intervene, which was hard for them.

Nausicaa used her dragon star skills then and creamed the five soldiers sent to restrain her. She did make it outside by picking up and throwing two Army dudes out the closed door. She made it outside and looked at Kerok, all forlorn in his crater.

One lieutenant took out his .45 and shot her three times in her stomach and chest. The colonel, running with the group (but staying well back of the violence Nausicaa employed) had this to say:

–No, no, you dumbass, don't shoot her. Just get some more guys and wrestle her down.

But it took more than a few guys. She recovered from being shot, the bullets did impact her, but didn't go through. Her body had three painful beestings, but nothing beyond. Nausicaa had at least a half-dozen glasses of dragon star blood in her. As she started to run out to see her companion, at least 20 soldiers attacked her. Nausicaa had her 'action-pack' on that would have excited Jing Chang and Sheeta Miyazaki. In the end, she defeated everyone, but killed no one. They knew they'd been in a bloody fight, that's for sure. More humans arrived, but they did not approach her.

Nausicaa Lee looked grim, as every-military-one-of-them *thought* she should. It was a sight to see: the rod was three-quarters consumed by the saurian. His arms, still rigid, hung down, his head and masseter muscle pointed skyward, like the rod had ripped the mystic life out of him. She didn't like how wide the mouth was around the massive rod. However, his many teeth surrounded the tungsten, grey entity and she noticed these were undamaged. That mere fact showed life had not fled the Alligatorian. The humans, meanwhile, were more concerned about how they could get the rod out of the deceased reptilian.

Now I'm ready to start my epic display. Give them a little hint!

Nausicaa dutifully turned to the Air Force colonel with a wink.

–If you killed a dragon-star, I'll eat *your* Air Force hat! With a terrific helping of ketchup, no less!

The two dozen humans looked on with awe and shucks, witnessing the strength of this 'weakest' saurian.

His large golden and silver eyes of-a-sudden opened, and his massive bulking arms rose up. Kerok's sizeable claws grasped the rod. The hypersonic device distended his heavily toned abdominals, which snapped back to their original, toned bulk when he pulled the whole thing out. The saurian lifted the 2,000 pounds up with a trove of strength, posing with it to the quiet delight of the onlookers with one massive hand.

–Now, my delightful humans, watch me make a lemon out of this vile thing!

Then Kerok bent the whole rod in half, in quarters, in 1/8s, 1/16s, 1/32s and so on, until this gross design was just a big kick ball. Then he crushed it down to the size of a small lemon. Then he made it flat, so that it was slightly bigger than an Eisenhower dollar. Kerok then tossed in up and down, like some gangster on a street corner, flashing a dollar coin.

–This concludes our time together, my military folks. I hope you've enjoyed it. I'm sure that most of your men, Russian and American will have some bruises, but they will heal. Since I'm one of the '47,' the weakest saurian out there, I hope you'll give a little pause to testing in the future. Especially when dealing with Crocodilians, a group you'll find a tad unfriendly, if you make the mistake of crossing them. I wouldn't do it, if I were you. They have a tendency to *melt things*. Just listen to their human companions, and you'll be alright. Sorry, I'm prone to giving advice, and you'd better take that, and I'll depart. My companion Nausicaa? Want a dragon ride?

Just then, he placed the 'dollar' on the hood of a HUMVEE. The reptilian squashed the dollar down and, subsequently, the tires crunched down, too. And since the ground was frozen in this section of Russia, they appreciably popped, one after the other. And quicker than a half-wink, Nausicaa boarded Kerok's back with a jump, and they were off. When the military human's reacted, the reptilian and his companion were 25 miles off (the forlorned base).

—Don't worry, don't worry, my human! The analogy of the 47 Ronin isn't lost on me. I heard you, and that completely. But my difference, at being the weakest of my overall race is not that severe. Look at your finalists of your muscle shows, your Mr. Olympia, say. You have 12 or 15 contenders, who finishes last? I'll be there, but I'm not that far behind my more 'developed' saurians. I'm normal looking, not in the 'top seven,' that is, Kukulkan, Teresian, Turinian, Larascena, Soreidian, Littorian and Korillia. They are all proud saurians. But I'm not among them, on the physical side. Give me a book, not an abs machine. Enough of this sinews shit, let's fly!

CHAPTER TEN

IF NOT HIM, THEN ME— ALL THERE IS TO IT!

TOWARDS THE END OF MY TIME ON EARTH, SOMETHING HAPPENED, quite out of the ordinary. All the letters, phone calls, text messages, twitter-mix, .htmls, URLs, all media, I didn't (really) answer any of it—except for one letter. One letter, I did answer. Thing is, it had a dragon on it. The puerile dragon displayed a banner saying, "Dragon lovers unite!" This stamp-image decried the saurian 'master-class' the incredible muscles and 'showiness' most saurians had (had). More incredibly than all of this was the declaration in bold type on the back (obviously it was a STAMP of some kind) you have: NOT TO BE USED FOR BRIBING POLICITIANS. Also, another STAMP, with a rabbit in a teacup, tickled me. Here is what it said:

Dear Brian!

Quite obviously, you get (several) letters every day! As a reader, you want folks to get <u>right to</u> it, no background, so, spoiler alert: <u>Brian Miller: Joan of Arc and the Dragon-Stars</u>—published in 2018, you can get it by typing in the same, on Google or any search engine. This is unique like Star Trek and Star Wars, only a (~~bit~~ whole lot) better! "Get Joan," it's only a hundred pages, and that's the explanation for the reasons <u>why</u>! Joan and the Dragon-Stars could sure use your help!!!

Thanks for the time!

J. Michael Brower
Writer
503.753.8325 <u>www.stardragons.org</u>

It was shocking! The guy was taking credit for <u>my</u> work! It was almost Hollywood, the criminality of it all, he was just plagiarizing what <u>I'd</u> written! It was criminal, beyond the pale, then, my soul-restored hatchet found this missive:

January 2019

Quite obviously, you like dragons—me, too! The 'dragons' in my seven books, this is my third or fourth letter to you, Brian, concerning my Brian Miller series. Now, I have to announce Brian Miller: Joan of Arc and the Dragon-Stars—published, as I told you, this year, you can get it by typing in the same, on Google, id est, your search engine. It's okay that you don't really respond to my 'scribbling pieces', my fountain-pen correspondence any-old-way. I think most people are in shock about my 'bad writing' (or worse). My wife says my writing is wrong, lousy, shitty, evil, a total annoyance, noxious, foul, rotten, shockingly boring, burdensome, and, in one word, just bad! It's very nice to have such loving support, but that's not my point. The thing is, *I'm possessed*! I had to write about Joan of Arc because Mark Twain and Bernard Shaw and a host of others wrote about her. Not that I'm in that "class" for writers—and that's the whole problem! I'm an anarchist in so far as I detest 'class' in all its colors. I'm a socialist, though, because people have to stick together—and I'm a Champaign socialist/communist because I embrace and celebrate President Roosevelt's Social Security system. This book, given its notes (all important), is really what I think (or there-abouts, soon to be confronted with its own antithesis, anon!). And, (at once) this is my weakest book to date. I know that. It took about a year to write, and I know the real weaknesses, hell, I wrote it! But, like one of my kids says, if "they" really like it, 'they' will just steal it from me. I'm sure you know about the pedophilias in Hollywood, so I'm prepared to have my shit stolen, who wouldn't be? I'm planning to do a Youtube.com series soon: I have to figure out how to edit stuff...of course, I feel estranged, abstracted, and really alienated from my work...but...here it is, here I am! (...won't you send me an angel?)—that's from the Scorpions (ahem, giving credit where it's due, which might not be my due!):

It was just *visions*, that's the answer to the question **??why??** creating my series of Brian Miller books. I've been a freelance writer and got paid to write. This is what Dan Cragg said, and that's how you can tell a writer—if he gets paid for what he's doing, that is, writing. He taught me that, but Dan almost always wrote with someone else (and, as you know, 'Brian Miller' and 'Harry Potter' have the same number of letters in their names, speaking of 'true things.' And I get 'Post-Truth' good in a note in Joan of Arc and the Dragon-Stars, too). Thing is, I met Brian Miller when I was a teenager, long before J. K. Rowling wrote about Harry Potter in her famous 'unemployment.' Because that's what happened, Joanne couldn't get a publisher in England, and everyone was very dismissive of her. Now, we know different. For me, I've gone through five publishers. That might be my epitaph. What I really need is a reply, and please, please buy some of my books! Thank you for your ideas.

Warmly Yours,

J. Michael Brower. 503.753.8325 www.stardragons.org

And another thing was emailed to me, that my clever hatchet[8] found for me:

Joan of Arc has tremendous imagery for me, and she's the start of my next book on Brian Miller. I'm sorry to again appeal to you, Brian. I also wanted to write you personally for this, but I wanted the information for what I'm trying to do to be clearly written; I have a tendency to be undecipherable with my script. You understand, I'm sure. You don't have to buy one of these books…but I still am doing this one on Joan of Arc. In the 1890s, Mark Twain wrote _Personal Recollections of Joan of Arc_ writing under the pseudonym of Sieur Louis De Conte. Clements thought it was his best book. But he wrote humor, and so disguised the fact that he penned it. I'm going to include the chapters here—all that's left is…to write it ;-). Please help me! Thanks!

Amazing, profound! Was that Samuel Langhorne Clemens? He didn't even spell it right! This is one of those 'diamonds in the rough,' little geniuses in the backwoods, not giving one-holy-shit about contacts or anything else. He's like Neil Peart of *Rush*—doesn't like 'fans' that much, "I can't pretend a stranger is a long-awaited friend," right? 'Fans' equal 'fanatics,' just for those egotistical enough to see it. Personally, I don't like Ayn Rand that much, Peart's little 'economic pet.' I could have set any saurian on him (not Peart, but J.

---

[8] This hatchet has a story, and it is told in Brian Miller Supplemental and Books II and III. Thing is, you 'expect' me to summarize what is going on with this hatchet in this book, presuming you read this book by itself. If it's that interesting to you, feel free to get the books for yourself!

Michael Brower) and that'd be it, or any Black World weapon, too. But I don't do that kind of stuff. It was the image that got me, not the nonsense he typed. The dopey dragon stretching out that banner, saying: "Dragon Lovers Unite!". Right away, I called the guy. He answered immediately, and I thought I heard him in a call center!

–Is this Michael Brower?

–It's been a while since someone called me that.

–So, this isn't J. Michael Brower?

–I. Am. That.

–Who has written about teenagers and dragons?

–Red hot, Doc!

–Well, this is Brian Miller, and it's a pleasure to talk to you!

–That's despite my candid (maybe forgivable) cynicism?

–The background noise has me thinking this is a call center?

–Nah, it's just the Bins.

–The what?

–Shit man, the Bins, the Bins (The Bells, The Bells!), just had to do a little Edgar Allan Poe on you, get it?

–You have lost me. Tintinnabulation that so musically wells, be shit-damned.

–Then permit me to find you. It's the Goodwill Bins, just look it up on YouTube.com, just everything (and anything) is stationed there! It's where all the failures go. What do you want?

–I got your letter!

–What person hasn't? I get my supply of stamps at the Bins. Steven Spielberg, Stevie Nicks, Stephen King, Trump, all the celebrities that have—

–You're not the guy in the red shirt, that I see on Youtube.com are you?

–I don't have a baseball cap, and that, never!

–Uh-huh.

–A hat might mess with my gorgeous locks!

–Touché

–There is a picture on my books, you have that?

–I have it now, thanks to my Black World sword, assisting me!

–So.

–So?

–So, what?

–So, come and see me, J. Michael Brower.

–Impossible for this reason: Economics, my friend. Bad economics. I'm afraid you'd have to give me a ride.

–Hold on. Clare, can you see to that, to get J. Michael Brower at the Bins in Portland, Oregon, here to see me? Yes, he's there now. You can? I'd be most and more grateful, your grace!

–What are you offering me, Brian Miller?

–A dragon-star ride, it'll be fun!

–You've got to be shitting me!

–No shit, and she should be there by now, this is a real Lizardanian dragon-star here, so have some needed deference, my man.

There was a huge total silence on the phone.

The 'callers' or the 'customers' just when completely silent in the wake of the massive dragon ducking down to get into the sliding doors of the Goodwill Bins in Portland, Oregon. In a wink, J. Michael Brower was standing in my giant room. The sun was at its zenith, shining through everywhere. This room was 80% glass. It was brilliantly designed, by the enterprising Black weapons. Clare's benign reptilian talons were off of Michael, that in a fury. The Black World Weapons lit-out and bowed to the visitor upon leaving. I looked on with some pique. The visitor looked grey, fat(er), slow, but had an eerie calm about just <u>being there</u>. I was in terrific shape (in fact the prospect of leaving the Earth had me feeling better than ever). This distressed me about my visitors' dilapidated condition. He looked around the room and noticed Clareina, standing by the window, preparing to go. Michael looked at a chair against the far wall and indicated it with a nod. Curiously she brought the chair over, a trivial affair, and placed it before Brian's desk.

–Thank you, my esteemed lady.

The Lizardanian smiled and then flew out the window and

didn't dent or destroy anything. That was a relief to the Black World weapons. Michael didn't just sit in the chair; he slumped and placed his hands meaningfully down beside him. He shook his hands briefly but vigorously.

–How do you feel?

His brown eyes looked quite a bit drunk. Just then I didn't know why. Later, I learned that he, too, had a stroke! I remember how I felt when I had mine on the Water World. I was scared. Right scared. Maybe Michael was flabbergasted with his first ride on a dragon-star, I don't know. He responded as well as he (really) could.

–Tired.

–I just didn't think you'd be, well—

–Old?

–Something like that.

–I am that. I've had a stroke, high blood pressure, seizures, oh, and I get sick (a lot). I'm sick now, can't get my breath. I don't want to tell you all my problems, you've something else to do today.

–I'm sorry, but maybe I can change that—

–It's too late for me. And you can stop dangling your modifiers all over my face.

–But the star dragons can—

–Nah, fuck it, let's not talk about me, let's talk about you.

–Well, first of all, Michael, I've some fervent questions and—

–Me first, my questions first?

–Seeing as I'm your host and you are my guest; I think that I should go first and—

–Paper, Scissors, Rock? And no probes, either?

This was fantastic! It's as though he was reading my mind, and yet he wasn't.

–Alright old man! Let's do it!

And I knew I wouldn't win. I could just feel it. Since I was strong as so many herds of Oxen, I thought about pounding out a fist, a Rock! He was crafty, I felt that. Michael was so calm; I didn't know which of The Three he'd produce. So, I pulled Paper! He responded, at the same time, legitimately, with Scissors.

–Shit-in-a-bucket.

–I ask first, and I'm going to throw some hardballs, Brian.

–Ask away.

–If I've the time.

–You think when you're dead it's over?

–Geez, I hope so, Brian Miller!

At that I had to laugh. I've been told I 'brought the house down' when I laugh. Still...

–Jay, really, these divine creatures can affect—

–I know what these creatures can do, and I'll ask the questions first, and call me Michael—that's best!

So, I shut my trap up tight. I sat back in my 1930s chair, the kind you'd see in the old-fashioned court room and brooded over my obscure, rather ridiculous guest.

My lodger wasn't interested in the angelic setting he was draconically 'brought to.' The whole outpost he just dismissed. Michael was disinterested in the intricate design of the Black World weapons, the artistic architecture of the entire place he just gave the traditional blow-off. The extreme glass background didn't catch his eye at all. It was a magical thing to me, really. Michael couldn't hear word-one, and I forewent the tour I was going to give him. He'd won the Paper-Scissors-Rock contest, so I was stymied. It was as though he already recorded it, somewhere. The majesty he just couldn't have got right, however. I had never seen such structures in my young life—the Black weapons even went around the world, bringing back wood of a terrific kind. Things from Australia and redwoods (even live ones) all around him, yet his indifference was extreme! Too many distractions, (too many destructions in his morbid mind) his time was very limited. I wasn't going to let him die, I cared for him immediately. We just met, and he had me at sixes-and-sevens. I played with the idea of telepathy with him. Michael just waived me off.

–Forget it, and no probing now, I mean it (and does anybody want a peanut?)

I smiled and looked down, also in a friendly manner. He was referencing The Princess Bride now, a line by Andre the Giant.

–Okay, Fezzik, you win.

–You and I share the same feelings, really, Brian.

–Feelings about what?

–We are both becoming dragon-stars, in our own way.

–Michael, I'm sure, that you are crazy; aren't we both humans, limited by our nature?

–I am that. Crazy and old. Thing is, I'm here before you. Just before we get started, I hear they will make you a dragon, right?

–Right again. I think I'll be saying that a lot.

–Just a for-instance: I overheard that you've been marked.

–Marked?

–That's right, with a dragon, no less.

At this, I got up, and revealed my arm.

–Thanks, and I knew it, now on to my questions.

–I hope they will be brief.

–As any woman's love. Shakespeare there for you.

I was aching for my series of questions, but he' won the Paper, Scissors, Rock contest.

–Just one thing, could I see your Black World sword?

Gingerly, she came over from her hiding place against the far door, looking J. Michael Brower up and down. Obviously, he wasn't a threat. I just stayed quiet.

–In my office, I've got—

No, just telepath with me, it'll be easier, quicker.

In ten seconds, she resumed her hiding place.

A valise was at Michael's foot. I responded curiously.

–What's that?

–My questions, all. Then, I'm done.

–A-ha.

–Take On Me?

–Huh?

–Oh, nuthin, just a little throwback to the 1980s. To my questions, please?

–You're dime.

–You got it! First, this initial book, <u>Brian Miller & the Twins of Triton</u> it's—

–I thought people needed an introduction, it's about two teenagers that save the world and—

–Now, now: I'll ask the questions, please?

Brian sighed and shrugged.

–Peacock Press of Pasadena? And do you ever get in contact with Karen E. Kapland?

–I know as much about them as you do. Just look it up on the Internet(s). It's all capitalism here, and that's the only reason they'd talk to you, it's all business, business and lies are one. That's why we are leaving. Next question?

–Hey, that's a good picture of you on the front, right?

–You'd have to ask Ms. Kapland.

At that, we were profoundly interrupted!

Knock! Knock!

The tremendous noise made me jump from the interview.

–Say, Brian, can I interrupt for, oh, an hour? Say that's okay, my little charming human?

Clareina, the Lizardanian, at my open door, and she had a huge mirror, of all things.

–So, what's up, Clareina?

–That's Clare! I need to debrief you (ahem), among other things. If you have any briefs on, and I don't think you do, very good!

–Yes, my noble queen Clare. Must be for my Soreidian-based nightmare, Michael. Can you excuse us for an hour?

–Oh, yes, I can, then my questions continue, Brian?

–You got it; my female Black World sword can bring you around the whole camp (or 'club' according to Joan of Arc), which will soon be in human hands, now can she?

–Sure, absolutely. Come on Michael, be with me?

Michael responded, got up and was one with the touring sword.

–See you in an hour.

It was just me and Clare. The way she 'sat me down' in my office, was literally her on top of my tender lap! A muscled enormity that I naturally put my arms around. Of course, I couldn't match my hands, and I awkwardly looked at her gorgeous, pouting abdominals. Normally, my femurs and 'general' hips would be crushed by my stunning Velociraptor-wife's sitting style (of course!). Taking 1,000 pounds of mega-sinews might sound a little titillating, but my fledgling teenage bones couldn't take it. How-some-ever, I'd binged on numerous wine glasses of blood by Larascena, Littorian and my now-bouncing saurian wife on my hips. That's right, I bounced Clare lovingly, gently, up and down, the pressure on my thighs, moderate, never taking my perceptive orbs off her massive silver, golden eyes.

–I've an animation-of-love for you that is yours particularly. I hope I can re-animated permanently. I'd die for you, Clare, but that's just the start of it all. I literally worship you but just let me get going! Your physical self no one can beat, even Lara isn't as defined as you are. All your muscles are steel, just having you on my lap is—

At this, Clareina turned around, shifting her huge position to be a rider on my burgeoning loins, which were out of control. I could feel her magic, and, indeed her hands on my generous junk.

–My lap is where it's all-at, my human.

–And my love for you is divine, I huddle with bowed head at your talons. Your great, iron breasts are—

Wordlessly, Clare ripped a giant hole in my robe, exposing my vast generosity, my angry, reaching head, bulbous.

–You were saying? Come on now, I'm here to be entertained and genuflected to, speak on! Just let me get this marvelous Clydesdaleian

91

device inserted, ah, their it (all) is. Yes, yes, fill me with that super-manhood, all the way up. I'll make my magical enhancements on your thick hammer, but not to the point of giving me pain. I know how much girth I can take. Pleasure will be mine, while I judiciously debrief you! Why did you interfere with me punishing Soreidian, and that goodly?

Then, not waiting for an answer, she ended the lap dance with a little wink, rose and stood by the chair.

—I've an idea, my horny husband, and it couldn't wait until tonight session. Oh, I'm going to debrief you, alright. See, I'd like you to get some sleep after that run-in with Soreidian. I can tell you, I wasn't prepared for his shenanigans, but no matter! I've something that is guaranteed to relax you, I just thought of it!

—I'm dying to be of extreme service to you, Clare, really.

—But it is I that can be of extreme service to you, my lucky sprite!

—Hey, a Sprite Dragon is in your field, I think.

—Wow, each time I talk to you humans you act much more bizarrely! Well, I could be married to a Sprite as well as a human.

I thought to my woman-wife-saurian-serpent, all drunk with her touch.

You could crush cities, waste armies to ruin, earthquake whole nations, with these exquisite ultra-arms! Oh, please make that Himalayan bicep peak stand up straight, I love to feel the thickness of this exquisite, rocky, warm, boulder-like arm.

I had at least 19 inches into her remarkable warmth, with a girth that exceeded any Pringles can, and was at sixes and sevens, just looking on like a stallion in generous season. Then, she took a claw out, the index finger, and waved it around. Having a super-Velociraptor doing this would cause fear in any person. Not me, however. I fidgeted on my desk, not knowing. Then, I heard the chair strain. The reptilian, all eight feet of her, rose while holding on to the chair, with just her left index finger. Her big boots were still on, and these black leathers were extremely sexy. The boots were at attention, then, they started to rise, all 1000 pounds, and the Lizardanian was smiling at me as I thought the chair would collapse. It did not, probably 'propped up' by her magic. Was it her magic or just Clare's sense of physics, your guess would be as good as mine.

Her tonality was complete, all physical muscle, totally maxed. Clare's bulging biceps were nearly 60 inches across, and almost that big around, pulsing with her wonton power. Then, she performed in a pattern of strength, all in this vertical position, doing all kinds of tonal exercises! Then she stood up via the chair completely, all in brilliant sinews. It was fantastic, and I creamed all over the bottom side of my desk looking in awe at Clare. Her subtle pulses, it was vigor, robustness throughout. I almost raised the whole desk up at the sight of this serpentine minx.

After this, my desk tittering on my angry destroyer, Clare flashed over behind my back, my eye darting in surprise. Then she had her way with me (as though anything prevented her). Her claws found my flesh and all-in with her many ministrations.

The kindly claws and hands proceeded to lift me off my feet, and over her elongated spikes, a full 11 or 12 feet up. Clare had a hand on my loins and my chest, which one hand covered almost completely.

–Oh, no, relax, relax. This is for you, now.

–Your intentions are, my mighty empress?

–You'll soon see!

The saurians whole body was skewered by my angry redwood tree. The ultra-appendage extended internally about three-quarters of her entire, chiseled body. All Clare's iron organs squished back by my massive tree trunk, cascading down her throat, threatening her stomach. Her excited, now leaning-in, organs felt like an ultra-tight womb, pleasure throughout. Clare insisted on taking on everything, the 'whole boat,' which she designed as both my veiny bowling balls, my shaft, and my obscene root in her dislocated, toothy maw. That done, my mammoth horsehead passed through her stomach, making its Titanic way forcefully down.

–Goodness, Clare, all your organs feel really wonderful, but where is this all going to end?

I said it out loud, in a little whisper.

Her entire maw consumed to the breaking point, dislocation extended to a dangerous level, she thought to me.

Maybe at my scaly end? Now, I'm not 'enhancing' you, it's Larascena's prolonged magic. Isn't that amazing? That's not an organ you've got in my mouth, that's a muscle I'm consuming. Let's just get that straight, (so to speak). We can use that muscle, making it stronger and stronger. Soon it will lift up a saurian, 1,000 pounds of dynamic muscle. And at this point, maybe a lot more weight, really. I'm talking about off the floor, like, my legs around you, in a perpendicular way. It'll take some mighty work to make that shaft-muscle sufficient, you know. Almost all Lizardanian's can't do magic, but Lara has taught me some sexual tricks. I don't know if I can take that giant python, it'd be fun to find out. And, hey, what do you think that mirror is for, now you can see why it's three inches deep, all around, the glass fixture going all the way around it, you know what that's for! I'm going to make you bust the most awesome nut you've ever, never seen, this will be so fun, prepare for exquisite awesomeness!

My three-times-stallion-sized member clouded its way down, me over her fins, stroking those biceps like air to breathe. I rammed it home but couldn't get those last inches into her. With her relaxing, I could see my irate mushroom causing an abdominal bulge, through her massive chest, bouncing those abs forward, and going down. I pumped the Lizardanian like a machine, splitting and grinding, sawing my way into her stomach and more. Obviously, she was extremely tight, the further I went down, the iron organs moving over like my destroyer was a veritable icebreaker. I had never felt such intensity. My bludgeoner was just about to go off! Suddenly, I saw my twice-fist-size shooter emerge out her backside. I was aghast, intrigued, it felt so, so good. Then when my 'whale' hit her bottom, and through it, angry head looking to destroy, her tail got busy. She set up a rubbing motion underneath my mushroom that was fantastic. I couldn't help it anyway and felt the Lizardanians tickling tail unchain my legion, creamy ropes.

–Oh, geez!

Then, it began, it finished six and a half minutes later, the whole mirror, inundated. I felt my bangable, kick-ball size basket within the bottom of her throat. My mammoth grapefruits began to rope-fully ignite into Clareina. I was expelling all my giant stream, rapid in force, from my burgeoning, overpowering, apple-sized mushroom, its slit open to the size of a nickel. I creamed right through Clareina like a tapir pig or a bull elephant, with complete abandon, looking at myself in the mirror. Her tail, just under my mushroom, going back and forth, rapidly. I pumped her like a speed piston, looking at my cream filling the mirror. I was afraid it would run over the three inches holding my voluminous batter at bay. Her entire body was like a cucumber sleeve, and I enjoyed it fully.

The angry violence of my legion ropes came to an end, and then she lifted me out, and down on my Lizardanian boots. Clare's dislocated jaw resumed its intimidating, iron form and she smiled.

–I'm afraid you'll need a new robe. This one has a gaping hole and it's all jizz splattered. Too bad. Was it nice, my human?

–Oh, yes. Tonight, in an hour or two, I'll pay you back, and that, bigly!

–I'm looking forward. Wow let me pick up this mirror, it's got to be two gallons at least! We've got to clean up this office, let's get going.

The Dragon turned to the honey-filled office, preparing to pick up the mirror.

–Just a minute, if you would, please.

Clare was standing at her usual eight- or nine-foot height, thought better and knelt down before me. I saw into her huge, silver and golden eyes, shining brightly.

–You want me to be a dragon, a dragon-star?

–In time, in time, my husband.

–You cared for me, loved me.

–Like you've never been loved before, sort of a big thrill, right, my human?

–I never really understood, until right now.

–Another revelation, right? Hey, you know I can't be parted with you, never and none.

We Frenched for a many, many minutes, in an embrace so warm and sincere. Clare thought.

Yes, my frightened Universe, I'm going to keep him.

Three quarters of my hour consumed <ahem>, the Crocodilian ripped all of the just-replaced, vast window out in a huge, destruction of sharp glass. Just like a cannon ball striking through wood, the glass shards would have gone right through me, even with dragon blood in my veins. My hatchet, taking the leading place of my touring sword, was attentive, swatting away the glass shards, and I tried to disguise my nervousness with the cacophony going on all around me.

And of a faster-sudden, Morris Kesecker arrived! He was riding the female Crocodilian responsible for shattering my glass office. This Crocodilian I hadn't met yet, and she was female, of too-course. I'd seen them before on Crocodilia, like when we first got there with Tiperia and everyone else.[9] Morris hopped off the dragon, to greet me, trying not to step on the 1,000 pieces of glass.

---

[9] It's rare that I ever do this, but, since it's either my book or J. Michael Brower's (who really knows?), let me insert it here, from Brian Miller and the Alien Shore (book Three). If you're a reader of this series, forgive me, and just skip it. If not, here is a good introduction of when I did meet Crocodilian women: Chapter Nineteen. Crocodilian Times. Littorian's presence on the world of Crocodilia was quite awkward to the Crocodilians. It was a complete shock to the hosts, too. The majority of the Crocodilians hadn't been informed about Littorian's recommendation for Turinian, the heir apparent to the 'throne' of Crocodilia (not that there was such a thing, anyway, anarchy not withstanding). No invitation for the visitors could be found—it was a personal invitation delivered by the thought of Turinian alone. A week before, Littorian, the Lord of the Lizardanians, was found guilty of a host of crimes committed against the Crocodilian people. It was death by Crocodilian fire and definitely needed. This was Genotdelian's order. Now, the Lord of

the Crocodilians was dead. Littorian, his slayer, and his Fellowship arrived on Crocodilia just to see the sentence carried out? All of it could drive a Crocodilian bat-fire-crazy.

Within the Crocodilians, fire ground in their massive mouths. Even within the Crocodilian women, they longed to do 'apparent' justice to Crocodilia, and smolder this Lizardanian, Littorian, into tiny matter, blowing in the wind. Kerok stepped forward into the fray of doubt and anger.

There were at least 50 Crocodilians around them. They looked on with curious eyes. Some of them just pointed at the smallest of the Fellowship.

–Isn't that a human, just there? I've never seen one. Talk about the scrawny kind too, and, what, totally naked! There flesh touches the 'outside,' see? Look at the bare skin, so close to all the elements, well!

–Yes, that's what they look like! I've heard the stories. They are kinda short, aren't they?

–They've Black weapons, see there? Some are attached to the humans, you see? Do you know what that means?

The numbers of Crocodilians grew and grew. Tiperia, now reduced to a regular-sized human female, stood at the center of the Fellowship, and curiously peeped out, between the saurians. Kerok was a little out in front, appeasing the Crocodilians, who stood in wonder. Brian saw Clareina hesitating, along with Korillia, at her side. They both clutched their Black swords impulsively. For Larascena, the Warlord just had a 'warlike' look, and couldn't help it. Littorian was looking strong and calm, keeping his protective arm around Brian's shoulders. Teresian had a similar look, hugging Katrina closely.

Jing Chang stood nearest to the Crocodilians and would doubtless be the first burned up in the coming fiery deluge. Some Crocodilians had little puffs of smoke rising from their nostrils. This human stood alone, and that interested the Crocodilians to no end. This human looked, well, different, but to the Crocodilians, all humans looked the same. They did notice something, though, piquing their curiosity. The human had great canines, filed off, wolf-like, and she was smiling. She was also well-built, the look of an athlete. Any given saurian, facing a vivacious wolf, what would they do? They respected the strength of the wolf, even though inferior to their own. All of Jing's teeth were similarly filed down, emphasizing all four, long canine teeth. Her masseter muscles became inflamed also, as she bit down in a snarl. She seemed to growl at them, viciously, too. The Crocodilians, unafraid, just gawked at Jing Chang.

J. Michael Brower

–Hey, Brian Miller! Sorry I didn't 'drop' by sooner—hint,

It made them feel awkward, and they shifted their hardened bodies around. Brian never noticed Jing's teeth. It was a 'good look' to this human, though. The swords were getting a little nervous, too. They filed in a zone defense, now, with their intricate calculations. The Black Swords were out in front, the knives next, with the hatchets, huddled in a final redoubt at the (inevitable) end. Jing's Black sword and Clareina's tapped lightly on the legs of Jing, indicating that she should back up. Instead, Jing maintained her position, shooing both swords away. Both Black swords did a lip-smack, but stayed near the Asian. Then, Sheeta Miyazaki moved up, and stood right next to Jing.

The two insistent swords looked helplessly at the knives, now defending two humans. They were about to break position, giving way for two knives, Korillia's and Kerok's, to protect the rebellious Asian human.

Littorian's sword, the leader of the protective force, was really focused on doing a good job, didn't see who was approaching him, in back.

A whispered Crocodilian voice was heard, but only by Littorian's frightened sword.

–Seems like a lil' too many to kill, right, my Black sword—or are you just on flame duty?

The Crocodilian just laughed and put a hand on the guard of the sword. The sword jumped, but the claws gave way a second later and that willingly. The flames that so many Crocodilians could produce staggered the mind. All of it was imagined, though. Tiperia could offer some escape, but now she was a mere human, just looking out between the saurians in an infantile way. The crowds of Crocodilians weren't interested in a fight, they were just surprised and curious. The guests created quite a fanfare on the eve of the christening of Turinian.

The hushed speaker, much to the relief of the leaders of the group, was Turinian.

Quickly, Brian took advantage, his white hair wavered back.

–Jing Chang, come here please. You ready? Oh, there's no time for a negative reply—you seem ready. My lord Turinian, future Lord of the Crocodilians, here is my gift, as promised, to you, on the Loreleian world! This is Jing Chang, of the People's Republic of China.

Turinian, honored, pushed benignly through the crowd of Crocodilians.

–And what is this, my friend Brian Miller Human? These are women, yes? One of your males would have been weak enough, but you're just giving me girls? My, you challenge me.

Sheeta stayed silent and had a calm assessment of the whole situation. Jing didn't care about the size of the upcoming Crocodilian. He was nearly 10 feet tall, had two five-foot scales running down his prodigious back, tapering at the end of his lengthy tail, arms the size of her legs, times two (or three, four). Big and brawny and not an ounce of fat could be seen on Turinian. Jing was prepared for this, and then some. She furtively looked at his long legs. His quadriceps had no equal, even among the Fellowship, and his gargantuan calves were spread out to an alarming circumference. He caught her looking at his legs and then smiled.

Without a word, Jing summoned her Black Sword, in her left hand. She did a karate-type pose with the sword, and her two hatchets and knives took their places on the ready line, poised for a fight, floating a little way behind her. She summoned up something else, her incredible élan. Jing knew she'd be challenged, knew it in the training time, in the Everglades, with Alligatorian and Lizardanian teachers. It was a tough, tough training course. Brian initially doubted that she could make the grade, but she did. All of the Middle Kingdom, on Earth so far away, was looking at her, awaiting this Chinese girl to make good with the star dragons.

Can a billion (plus) people be wrong?

Jing would see that they <u>weren't</u> wrong.

She could become a Companion, maybe the top Companion, and a Companion to a race that hated humans on account of the Twins of Triton. Jing would see peace reign across Crocodilia, no matter what. She knew what happened to the 30, and she visited the graves on one of her many (super-fast) jogs. She discussed it on the Black World, with the sword she held in her willing left hand. The sword, a male, understood, and knew her heart-felt feelings.

The Crocodilians were responsible. No one could, wearing the human design, resist a Crocodilian onslaught. Knowing all of this, Jing stood before the heir apparent.

–I can see nothing is a challenge to you, my lord. It is obvious why you rule this world. Would it trouble you, my lord, to have a sparring session with me now?

She said this in Crocodilian—which was burned into her in training by the Lizardanians (while she did innumerable push-ups for them). The Alligatorians, as was their wont, didn't study the Crocodilian language as intently as the Lizardanians. They relied on Universalian, and then left the matter alone.

hint! You kinda keep this place a mess, wow. Damn, this dragon-Crocodilian-star blood is better than anything on Earth. I'm sure glad we're leaving, it's not safe for us to be here, you cool with that? Man, I've something to telepath with you, geez, get this!

Morris had sandy hair and was really built. Obviously, his dragon-star was very content with this teenage companion. At that moment, he had a mental story to share, which just blew me away. Talk about a 'way' to introduce yourself!

CHAPTER ELEVEN

MOTORCYCLE, THE DRAGON AND MORRIS

MORRIS RECOUNTED THE TIME HE HAD WITH ISRAFELIAN, AND IT was so fun and done, I decided to put it down. Incidentally, Morris noticed my 125 Honda leaning against a tree outside. I said he could have it. And good, too. The 125 brought painful memories to me. Now this is hot stuff if you're a teen male (or female, really). I know you aren't used to hearing about teenagers and dragons, eight seconds be shitted on. His telepathy is here, in parts. It's "of passion" so be cautioned. The more <u>extensive</u> version, not shown here, reminds me of, well, <u>me</u>!

Israfelian was powerful, her muscles bulging on the post-Velociraptor, standing at just over 11 feet tall, but that's just the preliminaries of my most recent liaison, so let's get to it, Brian, and get ready. My dragon-star wished her three glasses of blood would pay off, draining them into me for three days. I was one of those restless teenagers that defied the '8 second rule' on sex, sorry to say, Brian; I'm at 4.5 seconds! At 17, sandy, long hair, fit, I thought persuading and pursuing women was just inevitable, for me. As a companion, I left human girls all behind for saurian women.

I got started, and that right away. The scene was on Crocodilia in Terminus's castle. You remember him, right, Turinian's second? Terminus had us as guests, he was off with Sheeta, going back in time to rescue Joan of Arc. Israfelian stomped her size 38-inch monster boot, denting in the wood.

—You will bring the wild saurian woman out of me, companion?

—And you'll bring the wild man out of me, Israfelian, my dear dragon?

—We'll see together.

—Really, Israfelian?

—Isn't it my love you were hoping for, as my companion? I felt it coming on in your person. Marriage, of course, <u>should</u> be like murder. You know the other person and it's over when you're dead. Of course, you'll live forever, and divorce is possible. Getting 'divorced' from a Crocodilian when you're a companion I just don't see happening. How could a human woman measure up to me, anyway? You have one question, <u>how</u> will you express it, that is, your love Morris?

—Express it? Maybe like this, perhaps.

At that, I walked up to the 11-foot-tall creature, and put my hands on her strapping forearms, and other places. Her heart was raised, and she smiled. The vastly muscular serpent, liking my touch, and wanting more, responded warmly.

—I need you, Morris. I want you totally. I just want to exercise all my strength on you.

I was apt to the call, to really 'know' (Biblically) a dragon. The excitement was soul-ridden and spoke to all the reasons for living.

—I'd be delighted to know your incomprehensible, almost God-like, power. Maybe our symbiosis can be continued, if you've got a mind too, my dragon mistress.

—Maybe we can move on, with your permission, my human.

—Move on to what, my gracious sovereign?

—Move on to my magisterial bed, of course. It might be a borrowed

bed, but it will have to do. This way and that, I'll have just enough time to do what I think you need done. I've learned no magic spells in general, but I've adopted one of Lara's spells just for you. What with your pawing me, maybe you'd like to go a bit further, and, um, deeper? Maybe I could give back?

I went into the huge bedroom, and, since we didn't know one another's bodies, the Crocodilian had some exploratory ideas.

—So, my dragon-star, what must I do?

—Enter my chambers and find out!

I didn't move away from the Crocodilian, I moved toward her. In not-so-secret, this is just what I wanted, violating the saurian's personal space. This reptilian didn't waste any time, and gently handled me like a mammoth girl playing with her own keep-sake Ken-doll.

At this, in a fit of erotic passion that I just couldn't help, I fondled and mauled up and down the incredible, puissant abdominals of the Crocodilian.

—Go ahead, my little human, paw me up and down, yes, yes, be a man in me (and, really, try to be dragon-esque!).

I marveled at her chiseled muscles, they felt like bubble wrap caked in any solid cement. Even the super-veins in her arms resembled titanium, but they strangely pulsed in an undulating way. I counted ten Atlantean structures, the bulk of the Crocodilian's abdominals, calling on me to suck very deeply. Then I did, and the saurian laughed slightly.

—We're going to exchange DNA, but I don't think we'll have a baby (yet!).

It occurred to me that this particular saurian could earthquake whole continents. Bringing me to raving heights of ecstasy, was just the stuff of child's play to this reptilian.

Already completely naked, disrobing me with clever and crafty claws, I was hoping for some necking, but Israfelian gently denied it. I was elevated, talons about my thin waist, light as any feather, by the cunning reptilian. Israfelian's permanent smile increased, the more I was lifted in her gentle clawed hands. There, raised up on-high, I was sucked by the Crocodilian, and felt the saurian's leviathan lower jaw on my bare backside, in a harrowing, but benign jawbreaker. My mind felt at home in reading the companion's thought-play. I was mesmerized at the super-strong, dualistic and turgid tongue engorged on my 19-inch, veiny phallus. And it was growing at an inch per minute.

—There's your essence now, how sweet and young, and honey slung, sure, and full of divine fun, looking to be mouthed and throated-out by a dragon, I'll hugely suck you, but good! Ah, yes, how 'bout this to start us out?

Israfelian's lengthy, forked tongue, over a foot long when she ran it out completely, cruised along my entire cucumber, aiming luxurious tonguing-action here and there, only on the super-sensitive spots, like under the fist-sized, mushroom-head. The ganderly tongue, twice as thick as my wrist, gently knew where to go. My swelling got bigger in the titanic mouth of this Crocodilian. Looking down at her equine face, I wasn't sure if a Percheron or a saurian was wont to give me pleasure, I was so alpha-male-top-dog!

—That tongue of yours, my God, it's a god, too! Geez, it's a luscious, tonguing gourd, it's wrapped around the whole thing. I'm going to girth-you-out, I hope your mouth can take all of this meat, Israfelian!

I shuttered in the Crocodiles' benign jaws, which only had eight inches to go before her scaled snout was at my abdominals. I lost count of the sinuous exquisiteness I felt on a continuous basis, being absorbed by this alien creature. I had Israfelian's masseter muscle in my shaking hands, fondling everything just because I couldn't reach the saurian's pouting and capacious, steel-like kettledrums.

—I sense you'll be coming (along) soon. The pre-tallow is making me think this to your mind. I have to get these last inches down; you are dislocating me, good boy! Lucky I'm a serpent, otherwise you'd snap my jaws open! My tongue fluttering can increase, see my human? I like your south-end very much, by the way. I can already feel your naked body trembling and quaking in my claws! Your divine monster is almost steaming, smoking in my mouth! That's appropriate for a dragon, too! Don't worry, I won't hurt you; you're in touch with my mind, so the

ecstasy you feel is registered in me, too. The liquid is going right in my throat, and down, it's so sweet, my companion. Boy, my stomach is filling up with your jizz, geez!

—Oh, Israfelian, my God, you're going past my very destroyer, oh geez, your tongue is wrapping around it, yeah, now I'm so crazy ded! *Keep going with this jarring, churning, meaty, tongue! Oh, God, I'm going to spend, get ready, damn, I'm almost there.*

—Wow, the spasm is increasing, my human. Your standing up tall, on my toothy face, just the position I want you sitting in right now; I want you to stay, riding as high in this sublime apex as you can!

The dragon-star then pumped and thumped me up and down on her giant, super-engorged tongue and mouth, thoroughly getting all the lifewater I possessed, damn I felt like a happy, overjoyed ragdoll, she was so strong! As a mighty star-dragon, the Crocodilian had no problem enveloping all my juices, immuring away without respite, no matter how many I violently spooged for the affair. It didn't fatigue Israfelian in the least; she could go on lifting me all day, if she wanted. Pining on high, I had both hands, on Israfelian's biceps, and my fingers didn't begin to cover those towering, and bulbous, peaks. The Crocodilian's tongue now bulged, and her two noses impacted my abdominals, in a gushing soup of passion, my teenager-goo going right down to ever-bloating abdominals. The saurian giggled with my sighs of pleasure, as I literally fed her all the contents of my kickballs. The 'Velociraptor' felt like a Triton among minnows, lifting and licking me, her claws overlapping my toned legs. Then, her curious hands wrapped around my chest. I then thought to the gorging reptilian.

—You've done it, I'm totally in you now. You're so strong, the girth so large, I'm just a mammoth King Clydesdale doing you! If you wanted, I could maybe belly-pop you?

—I don't think you could get through my scaly skin, but the thought is nice. I don't think any kind of gore would support us at all. No, I'll monitor you closely. I'm trying to be gentle. You like it, right, when I own your loins entirely like this?

—Yeah, I like it, intensely! Oh, deeper, deeper, I'm going to flood

your copious teeth and mouth with another soon-screamer, and I'm not embarrassed to say it.

Israfelian knew the place, monitoring my heaven-sent and sumptuous mind, where to stop before it became unpleasant.

I then roared, once again, myself, head flailing from side to side, crescendoing with abandon, fantasy-color cascades in my closed eyes, powerful internal contractions raising my bowling bowl gonads up and down, over and over again, surprising the reptilian. Still, the suitor didn't stop slurping on me. Then, after my loud roar, going on for five full minutes, rutting away with all my strength in the highest ecstasy, the reptilian, looking with her gigantic, glimmering eyes saw me totally spent. While still wobbling like a drunken sailor, she took my doll-like body in her powerful claws and laid me on the bed. Israfelian took an assessment of me, meanwhile sucking down my dripping yo-yos of lifewater, covering the Crocodilian's sizeable teeth, dripping down her muzzle. Then the saurian got into bed with me, nuzzling me over. She laid her head on my chest, knowing that the dragon-star blood in me would compensate for the weight. We rested on the bed; I was still breathing high-pitched gasps, then it settled down to relieved sighs. Damn, Brian, I almost albinoid her whole face. Israfelian had the locks of Sia, that's for sure, all dripping like satin glue down her mamahood and muscled chest, it was epic.

—That was indescribable, incredible! My turn, my most precious Crocodilian!

Then I stood up, and that's not all that was standing up, either. The Crocodilian, gamely enough, sat up expectantly, her tail involuntarily jumping around. Placing my thumbs out, with four fingers stretched along the reptilian's narrow totally muscled obliques, I lifted.

At first, the Crocodilian, wiping her mouth from my many angry juices, doubted I could lift her. After all, she was just over 1,200 pounds of complete, dynamic muscle. In this sense, Israfelian reckoned without the star dragon blood coursing through my veins. This weight was nothing to me, I could thrust her up all day, and she admired my biceps, her hands so warm, claws so cold!

I wanted to give back to the reptilian, wanted to feel her lifewater racing out, raining down my neck, over my toned, six-pack stomach, puddling on the castle's floor. Very much surprised by my efforts, she roared-giggled nervously, then grabbed my shoulders to steady herself.

—Wow, you do have a strength to you, boy! Ay caramba, as they say on your world, now, careful, you're going to enter my more sensitive area and...oh, oh geez, yes, hooowww, deeper, deeper...

I cooed at her response, right on target. Of the skin, or the scales, of the creature, I was most mesmerized. As I kissed it, here, there, everywhere, she felt warm and fashionably slick in my mouth. Plus, it was, all of it, muscle, just warm muscle, and I couldn't get enough of the Crocodilian's gentle scales. I placed my tongue on the saintly distension, now growing, and mouthed it violently. Then, I perceived a pleasant liquid, just beginning, as I sucked away at the clasping passageway.

—Your set-up like a woman, a human woman and I know just what to do with this *little tantalizing protuberance and I'll more than just nibble it, so don't crush my head with those powerful hands, right, my lady?*

I doubly went to work, sucking on the 'disturbance,' till it pulsed, quick and hard. The Crocodilian jerked spasmodically each time; my mouth encumbered by the scaly, juicy mound. The twelve-thousand-pound reptilian, with shaky, gargantuan hands braced on my shoulders, was completely at my mercy. I'd have no mercy, right then. Quicker and quicker, my tongue-lashing had no quarter, no respite. This was going to be the biggest Cyclops-crest yet!

—Oh, the gods; you little stud, you little mini-horse, you are an adoring angel, don't stop, don't stop!

I dutifully continued to suck away.

—I know you can't belly-bulge me, but your tongue is learning; keep going my little Clydesdale!

I could tell that Israfelian was violently awed at the strength of the star dragon blood within me. She'd heard the stories, about giving this Tree of Life to me, a human, but the power she was infusing in me was unbelievable. I was playing with the nipples tucked away under the muscled chest of the Crocodilian, just like an expert porn star, reaching up, I could barely touch them. I put my fingers on the cleverly hidden, but still meaningful-woman-lumps, manipulated them in writhing circles. My fingers registered the thrill this was giving the saurian. She moaned, screeched and "little-roared," all the time I pawed them. Israfelian was not paying attention to the sensuous fingering I was giving. All the Crocodilians' concentration was on her quim within my sensuous mouth.

–I need that orgasmilk cascading down your quim; I want it to flow over me, Israfelian! Come on and give it to me, give it, I'm here for just you!

After about ten minutes, my efforts paid-off super-big-time. The saurian had hold of my biceps, draping over me with claws which were so large, they lashed together on both sides of my toned upper arms. I thought that was fine but did not want to stop the tremendous licking as the reptilian straddled me, up-on-her-majesty. I then felt lustfully powerful, holding up the mighty dragon in ecstasy, given that the saurian was sexually mine, way up in the air, depending on me completely. I pumped her up and down, just for the thrill of it. After about two light washings, I thought this was going to be a big one, as the star dragon's furrow began wracking around in my mouth. I had, at that moment, to strain my lips a little. The Crocodilians' breathing momentarily stopped.

–The Gods, you're draining me! You've drained me, take it all, all of me, your ab-so-lut-ely draining-my-quiescence out of meeee!

Then a washing, a river of orgaswater, began really flowing, like a raging river, actually shot out of the reptilian's voracious, shivering passage. Damn, Brian, I was surprised that she could produce so much. The saurian roared loudly, out of control. I redoubled the grip on the saurian's muscled midriff, to manage her. I gulped the soul-flow down, and it actually tasted sweet, almost as good as her blood, the Tree of Life. And drinking the Tree of Life, I will live forever, and have the strength of gods, besides! I've been so lucky that Israfelian called on me to be her companion. The solicited milk seemed like it never would end, it must have been some minutes, and I didn't stop licking the whole time, sucking it right down. It flowed clear, over my body, down the front, an inch thick, pooling on the castle's floor. I then sucked deeper, wanting more of the nectar.

The dragon-star then felt weak in my extreme grip. The Crocodilian's sinewy abdominals began to rack around, my hands actually started to pulse up, the ab-sweet-agony was so strong, so I reluctantly stopped. The dragon actually felt deceased, sweetly dead, in my hands. Tickled and amused, but not worried, I knew that kind of sexual exhaustion quite well. My mouth remained transfixed to the reptilian's hairless-mound, now that it was dying, amiably dying, sending out only a trickle of life-milk. All the while, I guided the reptilian sweetly to the bed. Then, after a long time, with the dragon sublime and prone, I took my watering mouth off of the beast. I assessed the great and exhausted creature on the satin bedding, but still being lightly touched on her abs and chest by me.

—Wow, that was a giant, huge discharge, Israfelian! I think I got down all that lifewater, but there was so much of it! I'm covered with saurian yoyo-reptilian-woman-honey right now! I'd say it was two pints, maybe just this side of a gallon, all completely clear and just nectar sugared. You're a beautiful creature, for sure. That must have been a relief, right my companion, uh, can you talk now?

Breathing heavily, mouth open, the Crocodilian's eyes were tightly closed. Slowly, she opened them into slits.

—Oh, you said it there, Morris. Gods, I never knew my crowning point could be so good, so long, and now so relaxing. For me, however, I'm gonna keep you; don't make a move Universe, this human is, indeed, mine!

A ferry boat's worth of fruit and wine awaited us, she didn't skimp on refreshments. We partook of all, laughing, feeding it to one another, man, she is a companion for all time.

At the end of his thought-pattern (and it was lucky I was sitting for that one, I had an iron woody, damn), the Crocodilian, now out-of-doors, wrapped her tail intricately around the 125 Honda, and picked the motorcycle up, quite effortlessly. I waved to her, with approval. She was monitoring our mental conversation the whole time, and Israfelian nodded to me, and flew off, Morris on her muscled shoulders.

CHAPTER TWELVE
ALL THERE IS TO IT (TWO!)

–HEY, CAN I COME BACK IN, BRIAN?

In a new Alligatorian robe (the old one had inevitable stains, and was taken away by my attentive knives, the whole area, cleaned up, with Dragon Blood incense burning), I motioned my writer in. Clare left, just then.

–Until tonight, right Brian? Remember, eight seconds…

Night would have been in two hours. Clare laughed hysterically.

–Did I interrupt something, Brian?

–There is no interrupting her.

–Let's continue with my queries. Wow, Katrina's name, Katrina Ivanovna Chakiaya, that's a mouth full and—

–Seagull.

–Huh?

–Her name, it's 'seagull' or 'bird' in Russian, I guess.

–Well, there are a lot of misdirections, spelling mistakes, syntax errors, you leave Strunk & White in any cum-dumpster fire and—

–I had a woman helping me with the first books, Rosemarie Skaine and—

–Where'd you meet her?

–I never met her.

–What?

–I've never met her, and she is dead now. She was a sociologist and a very, very honorable woman. As a matter of fact, I'm thinking about bringing her—

Immediately, Brian's eyes darted to Clare's exit, and to the skies, beyond, maybe looking for dragons.

–Let's get into the Twins of Triton.

Brian looked over.

–Let's not.

–Just a little?

–Oh, just go ahead.

–M'kay. Robert Brodsky, wow, there is a character.

–He's real, or he was.

–Who is he?

–He came from Russia, changed his name to 'Brent' and tried to 'assimilate,' he was a Jew. He was a writer; aren't we all?

–I'll ask the questions, now, Brian.

–And I'll elude them. Next?

–Geezum-hood-crow...what's that mean?

–They say that in Vermont. It's just 'surprise,' really.

–Uh, Homage to Catalonia...

–That's a book I still have, there it is, you can look at it.

Brian then brought it over, a paperback, yellow, with a rifle barrel and a bayonet on it, with a trickle of blood. It was on the floor, not packed up yet for the move off Earth.

–Next boring question.

–This is boring?

–Oh, yeah.

–You'd rather be doing something else?

–Some<u>one</u> else, since my last visitor left, has it been eight seconds?

–Teen mentality?

–We have a mentality? That's new; I think we think with our loins, mostly, almost exclusively; just go on!

–Heroin?

–I've found the cure to that, too: My last visitor, for instance (and she's not the only 'for instance.'). Hey, that's enough interviewing for now.

And almost immediately, Larascena, the Warlord, bounded into the office.

–We will continue this another time, Lara, can you bring J. Michael Brower back to Portland, Oregon, now, he'll tell you where he lives, so please you? Oh, pay this guy out of the kitty, like, $100,000, if you so-please.

–But we haven't discussed all the other books, the fact that you mess up the names of the Alligatorians and the Lizardanians and the Crocodilians so much, and what is this "French Form" of writing, like with Anthony Burgess scribbling M/F, and this thing about the Saurian Theory of Anarchy and making fun of Nietzsche and Carcosa and this zombie thing with Kukulkan and in "Ink" with *What Happened to You?* and with Katrina and Joan of Arc who then—

Seizing the belletrist in her benign, good natured talons, stuffing a big envelope in his pocket, J. Michael Brower was so gone...until next time!

CHAPTER THIRTEEN

My Wysterian Update

It's Teresian, here, the Wysterian, and I'm going to, what, you don't want me to 'get on with it,' right here Brian? For why?

You don't want to have thirteen chapters?

OMG, what a pagan you are, Brian! Don't interrupt me on my chapter, like you did with Kerok on The Theory of Saurian Anarchy, okay? And you don't want a Wysterian mad at you, right? 'K. I will be brief, as any man's love!

CHAPTER FOURTEEN

ADVENTURES IN THE BUTTERFLY ZONE

FIVE OR SEVEN GOLDILOCKS PLANETS ARE IN THE VERY NEAR future for any human 'wanting a good time.' Point is do you trust me? Oh, of course you do! Sure, I'm one of the most intimidating saurians you're ever going to meet but wait 'til I get going!

I've got five planets that everyone and anyone can move to, like, right now! The other ones I'm just looking at, but these are in the butterfly zone. I'll move you guys out at, what, year to year? Transports will take anyone who wishes to go at, say, June 1st every year? I've got the places mapped out, and I think I've expressed those somewhere before. If you don't want to be here anymore, I can take you guys to a newer world, a much better world. You can mess it all up, just like you've done here. I don't care, as in keeping with anarchy.

Still, I hope you'll be environmentalists about it all, but I'm not counting on it. Minds, like souls and hearts, can change, that is, get new information; thesis, antithesis creating a new synthesis. This is all my favor to you, and I've got all the bulldozers, trucks, and settlements all established, just by my magic alone! And my <u>magic is permanent</u>, too. So, all of you right-wingers and left-wingers, well, there you go! Flourish and progress! Oh, I'm not God Almighty, either, but, as a dragon-star and a Wysterian, I can be embellished and genuflected to. Just anytime.

DER FINIS

Printed in the United States
By Bookmasters